WHIRLWIND MARRIAGE

WHIRLWIND MARRIAGE

Louise Armstrong

CHIVERS

British Library Cataloguing in Publication Data available

This Large Print edition published by BBC Audiobooks Ltd, Bath, 2007.
Published by arrangement with the Author.

U.K. Hardcover ISBN 978 1 405 64282 8
U.K. Softcover ISBN 978 1 405 64283 5

Printed and bound in Great Britain by
Antony Rowe Ltd., Chippenham, Wiltshire

CHAPTER ONE

The hairdresser stood back, gave a huge, beaming smile, and brandished her blow drier.

'There you go, honey. You're just beautiful.'

Paula Jackson picked up her tinted glasses and placed them firmly on her nose before looking in the mirror. When she saw that the glamorous face looking back at her was surrounded by a cascade of golden, highlighted locks, she let out a soft gasp of amazement.

'That's not me!'

The hairdresser's chuckle was rich and vibrant.

'You was in there all the time, honey. All it took was a little sunshine, a little tinting, a little tweaking here and there. You should keep up with the eyelash dye. It sure brings out the best in a blonde.'

Paula looked at her newly-brown lashes and eyebrows and had to agree. The darker lines gave her face an allure it had never shown before.

'I never go to a salon,' she confessed.

The hotel hairdresser touched the gleaming mane that flowed over Paula's shoulders.

'You wear that lovely hair in a plain old plait all the time? It's a crime.'

The hairdresser whisked off the pink cape. Paula got to her feet and smiled.

'You're a miracle worker,' Paula declared.

'All part of the service, honey. And don't forget you have a free aromatherapy massage to come.'

The heat was like a warm blanket on Paula's face as she left the air-conditioned comfort of the salon. As she crossed the beautifully-landscaped hotel gardens she could smell woodsmoke from a bonfire and the salty tang of the sea. Classical music drifted over from a rose-covered arbour where a bride in misty tulle was kissing her new husband. Two happy families cheered them on.

Paula had planned to go back to her room and read, but even through her tinted glasses, the white sand was sugar bright and the water glittered blue. It was too beautiful to turn her back on. A restless feeling propelled her down the path that led to the beach instead. The silky sarong she was wearing was light and comfortable even in the heat. She could feel the unaccustomed brush of her hair as it flowed loose down her shoulders. She crossed the hot sand and then took off her sandals so that she could dabble in the cool wavelets at the water's edge.

Paula looked down at her freshly-painted toes, and then waved her hands in the warm air so that she could admire her gleaming nail tips as she walked. She had the feeling that someone would walk over and tell her she looked different, but she knew that was silly.

She was all alone on holiday, and no-one at Rum Smuggler's Cove even knew her. As she wandered farther down the beach, she wondered what it would be like to feel glamorous all the time, glamorous and liberated.

It was lovely to have so much free time. She strolled on idly, picking up pretty shells and turning them over to see the mother-of-pearl inside, dabbling her toes in the cool water, revelling in the unaccustomed holiday feeling. She must have walked for nearly three miles by the time she realised that she was hot, and thirsty.

Shading her eyes, Paula looked back along the beach. She'd walked right past the strip of hotels. The nearest one was just a white dot in the distance. A bead of sweat trickled down her face and the feel of the sun was like a hot, heavy hand pressing down on top of her head. She'd been foolish to walk so far without a hat, and now she remembered that she had no sun tan lotion with her, and her skin was letting her know it. She looked again at the distant hotel. She'd fry by the time she walked back there.

She turned around and looked in the other direction at more blazing white sand, hot blue sky, dazzling blue water. All very well for a holiday poster, but not what she wanted to see at this moment. The only patch of shade was under a clump of palm trees. She could see a couple of tables and sun loungers underneath them. As she crossed the sand and walked towards the shade, she could feel the heat of the beach striking up like the heat from an oven. As she got closer to the trees, she saw that one of the sun loungers was occupied by a magnificent specimen of male, lying face down on a blue towel that brought out his tan nicely.

Paula hesitated, looking at his muscled back doubtfully. He'd be sure to wake up if she went close to him, and then what would she say? She half turned away. She could walk back to her hotel. But then, on the table next to the sleeping male, she spotted a two-litre green glass bottle of water. She'd never wanted a drink so much in all her life.

Her body made the decision for her. She darted over the remaining patch of sand and dived into the shade. She felt cooler at once, but then she remembered that she had no money with her. She bit her dry lips and felt thirstier than ever, but she couldn't help herself to someone else's water, could she? As she stood hesitating in the shade, the long, lean figure of the man rolled over. Feeling oddly nervous and defiant, she looked down at his face. He smiled back at her with sleepy blue eyes.

'Hello.'

Paula forced herself to smile casually.

'Hello.'

He swung his well-muscled legs over the

side of the sun lounger and sat up and smiled again. Paula saw that the sleepiness had been deceptive, or perhaps merely temporary. The deep, dark blue gaze contained a sharp intelligence, and a lively electricity. She was instantly physically conscious of him as a man. A quiver of awareness shot down her spine. She wanted to look away, but she simply couldn't break the spell of his steady gaze, and then, when she registered the appreciative nature of his stare, she found that she didn't want to look away. No-one had ever looked at her with so much admiration before, and she found that she liked it. She liked him, and she liked him even more when he divined her needs at once.

'It's hot out there. Would you like a drink?'

Murmuring gratefully, she sank on to the next sun bed to his. Ice-cold water had never tasted so good. She grabbed the glass with both hands and gulped it so quickly that she got a pain in her forehead. She rubbed it and he laughed.

'Here, drink the next one more slowly, or I've a beer if you'd like one.'

'Just water, please.'

Ice tinkled as he rummaged in the cool box that stood under the table. This time he filled the glass with chips of ice before pouring. Paula took the glass and relished the cold feel of it between her palms.

'Thank you! I walked much too far without

realising it.'

His eyes met hers seriously.

'With pale skin like yours, you certainly should be careful.'

Then he stopped and gave a devilish grin.

'There's nothing like Caribbean sunshine to make people reckless, is there?'

Paula dipped her head in agreement, and a sun-coloured lock of hair tumbled over her shoulder, brushing at the bare skin, reminding her what a different image she was presenting that day. She looked different, and she felt different. She was a sexy-looking woman who walked alone down tropical beaches and met with strange men. The imp of temptation popped into her mind. She fluttered her eyelashes and decided to flirt a little.

'Reckless and fun-loving.'

An electric shock seemed to zing between them, and the man spluttered on a mouthful of water.

'Wow! Are you?'

Paula was a little afraid of the reaction she'd created, but only a little. Flirting was fun, and she had to admit he was gorgeous. She looked directly into his eyes and smiled warmly.

'I'm certainly in a holiday mood.'

He sat bolt upright and held out a strong, warm hand.

'And I'm the man to help you enjoy it. I'm Mike—er—that is, Sebastian Kent is the name.'

'And I'm Paula, er, I mean Charlene, Charlene Jackson.'

'Are you here with a friend, Charlene?'

Paula nearly told him how Sally had broken her ankle the day after they'd paid for the holiday in full, but then she stopped. Would a woman called Charlene need an excuse to travel on her own? She gave a shrug.

'Oh, I often take a Caribbean break at this time of year.'

He looked rueful.

'February in England, don't I know it. You are English, aren't you?'

'One hundred per cent. I come from Manchester.'

His dark blue eyes glowed.

'So do I! Charlene, this was meant to be.'

He was flirting right back. Ridiculous! She hadn't expected to find herself in the middle of a flirtation! She was an accountant. She worked five days a week, did her chores on Saturday and had dinner with her parents on Sunday. She'd never been to the Caribbean before, let alone talk to such a good-looking man. There was a star quality about him that Paula couldn't help responding to, but she felt her cheeks flush. He was out of her league.

Sadly, she took a sip of her drink and looked out at the glittering blue line of the sea, then she looked back at Sebastian. The gently-rustling palm trees threw soft patches of shadow over his face. His blue eyes were very

7

vivid in his lightly-tanned face. Although his straight dark hair was clean and glossy, he hadn't bothered to shave that morning and a slightly dark shadow gave him the raffish air of a pirate! And yet despite his glamour and stunning good looks, Paula sensed a pleasantness about him, as if he were a favourite big brother that you could always depend on. She felt a deep tug of regret in her heart.

'Thanks for the drink. I'd better be getting back now.'

He sprang to his feet and put out a hand to stop her.

'No! You mustn't go!'

His hand was large and dark on her bare white arm. Paula hadn't realised how big he was, how well-muscled. She forgot her earlier impression of niceness and noticed that he towered over the top of her head. She remembered how deserted this stretch of beach was. Fear, sharp and primitive, dried her mouth. He was looking directly into her eyes. He must have sensed her anxiety, for he let go of her arm and stepped back at once, although his voice remained urgent and pleading.

'Have dinner with me, tonight.'

She wanted to. Not every man would tempt her, but a secret thread of desire seemed to draw her towards him. Excitement fluttered in the pit of her stomach and she felt a surge of exhilaration. She would play at being a glamorous vamp a little longer. She looked at his face as she answered.

'OK. My hotel or yours?'

She saw his eyes warm, and smile at her repartee as he answered.

'I'll pick you up at your hotel and then take you to mine! I want everyone to see how lucky I am.'

She couldn't think of a smart reply, so she merely glided away over the hot white sand, hoping that she looked more poised than she felt. Had she really picked up a man and arranged a date? But she hadn't told him where she was staying! How would he find her?

CHAPTER TWO

By the time the sun was low on the horizon, Paula was too restless to stay in her room any longer. There was no-one waiting for her in the spacious marble of the hotel lobby, and she was too shy to ask the desk clerk if anyone had been looking for her.

She slid open the glass doors that kept the hotel air-conditioned and stepped out into the lushness of the thick, tropical air. Candles and white tablecloths fluttered on the dining terrace. A waiter smiled at her, but she mimed to him that she was going for a walk before dinner. She had no doubt that she'd be eating alone, later that evening.

Down on the seashore the breeze was even stronger. Her tropical-print dress blew in the wind as she walked. The first clouds Paula had seen in the Caribbean sky massed on the horizon, turning gold and then pink and then crimson as the sun set. She could see the wedding party again. They were posed against the romantic backdrop and the hotel photographer was snapping busily.

Paula felt very alone as she carried on down the sand. She could hear music and laughter, smell the beach barbecues getting ready for the evening. It seemed like everyone was with someone, except her. In an effort to break her self-pity she kicked off her sandals, lifted her dress over one arm and waded into the silky water right up to her hem line. The setting sun threw a glittering path of orange across the waves. She was so lucky to be here. How much more did she want?

'Charlene!' an irritated male voice snapped behind her.

Paula heard splashing behind her and a strong arm grabbed her wrist.

'Charlene, where have you been? I thought we were having dinner tonight.'

She spun around and saw six foot of annoyed male scowling at her. Sebastian had found her at last! She'd forgotten she'd told him that her name was Charlene, but the

10

fiction had its uses. Paula Jackson would have been intimidated by the hunk who was glowering at her from under dark eyebrows, but Charlene Jackson gave him a naughty grin and spoke cheekily.

'I knew you'd find me.'

He gave her a smile that showed sudden dimples.

'You didn't make it easy for me!'

He was still holding her wrist. Paula took a firmer grip on the fabric of her slipping skirt in one hand and swung herself nearer his body. She walked the fingers of her free hand up the front of his polo shirt.

'Am I worth it?'

Her whole body thrilled to the smoky, hungry look that moved in his eyes. She felt the power and the magic, and she knew why women loved to act like sirens. But, as she stood in the warm, Caribbean dusk with the sea tumbling around her bare legs, she also felt guilty. She could feel the special quality of the connection that was growing so quickly between them.

She wanted to look him in the eye and tell him the truth about herself. He deserved to know, but then that look of desire would dwindle and vanish, to be replaced by polite boredom when he found out that she wasn't a femme fatale who could charm and entice him, but an accountant with a fixed routine and her videos in alphabetical order!

11

She suddenly realised that he hadn't answered her. She tilted her head to read his expression and wondered what he was going to say to her teasing. He said nothing. He lowered his head and he kissed her. Paula tasted sea spray and madness and she let go of her skirt and clung to him tightly with both arms.

The rush of the sea was loud as it swirled around their legs. She felt his heart beating crazily under his shirt. She never wanted to let go of his strength and his serenity. His mouth was a promise on hers. Time telescoped around them. The silver tropical moon was showing over the rim of the sea by the time Sebastian lifted his mouth from hers, pausing to kiss her on the throat, the neck, the eyelids. He wrapped her long hair around his hand and kissed that. He looked at her face and spoke ruefully.

'What's happening to us?'

This was Paula's chance to break away, to mutter something sensible about a nice dinner. Instead she wound her bare arms around his neck and murmured huskily.

'Something wonderful. Something that's wild and rare and precious.'

He shook his dark head and traced the line of her lips with a gentle finger. In his eyes she could see the wariness that men show when they meet a wicked woman, but she could see, too, that he was captivated by the image she

12

was offering. If there was a war going on inside him, she was winning it easily. He looked at her with eyes that were dark in the moonlight, but a large wave came slapping out of the night and they both fell back laughing. He took her hand and towed her towards the beach.

'I think the tide's coming in.'

They separated momentarily to rescue their sandals, but Sebastian soon took her hand again. His grip was warm and secure, and it made her feel safe. Her dress was wet against her legs, but in the warm night it didn't seem to matter, and she shook her head when he asked her if she wanted to go back to the hotel and change.

'I'm too hungry to wait.'

They ate at the first beachside restaurant they came to.

This can't be me, Paula thought, as she nibbled at smoky, barbecued fish and delicious prawns hot from the grill. She felt as if she was living out a fantasy from a romantic movie. She knew she couldn't be in love. She'd met the man only that morning, but she'd never felt more alive, or happier.

The stars shone in a velvety sky, a steel band played a lament in the background. A silver cloud floated over the moon and she shivered. Sebastian noticed at once.

'Are you cold? I should have made you change that wet dress.'

The silky fabric slipped through her fingers as she flirtatiously touched his bare knees with the hem.

'It's already dry, feel it.'

He shivered as the fabric touched him, then swallowed hard and looked at her with open delight.

'What a creature of impulse you are.'

Paula lowered her eyelashes and raised them. She hardly felt as if she was lying as she made the pronouncement.

'I believe in living for the moment.'

He jumped to his feet and took her tiny hand in his own.

'Let's dance.'

The steel band played on and a big man took the microphone, singing of love. Sebastian gathered her up in his arms. Paula could hardly breathe, and not just because her face was buried in his shoulder. She'd never been held so tenderly by a man who looked at her with so much affection.

A pulse hammered at her throat as they danced into the night, his body seductive against hers. Sebastian had definitely taken the lead. He was moulding her soft body into his own. It was wonderful, tantalising, and it was very disturbing but she couldn't move away. The moment was too beautiful, too marvellous to lose. She snuggled closer. He murmured to her softly.

'You were like a shimmering flame on the

14

beach. I longed for you as soon as I saw you.'

Paula melted in his arms. She was so happy. She heard him laugh softly. His lips moved in her hair.

'I've never dated such a wild woman before.'

Paula tilted her head back and smiled at him dreamily.

'Maybe I'm not what you think I am.'

He held her close.

'Charlene, tell me not to kiss you.'

The golden purr in her own voice surprised her.

'Kiss me first, then I'll decide whether you should or you shouldn't.'

The kiss was pure magic and so were the hours that followed. They didn't stop dancing until the very last light was extinguished. A waiter approached them, smiling sympathetically.

'So sorry, we're closed now, sir, madam, but at the Hotel Blue Cavern you can find a discotheque.'

Sebastian settled the bill then drew Paula's arm through his and urged her to follow him along the white beach.

'Do you want to go to the Blue Cavern?' he asked.

She shook her head, listening to the wild roar of the surf.

'I'm not in the mood.'

He drew her close and they kissed yet again.

'Nor me. I'm glad we're in tune. All I want

15

now is to be alone with you.'

Paula met his eyes and felt shock right down to her toes. He was smiling the way men smile when they think they have won over a woman, and she knew that he expected her to feel the same way, and why wouldn't he, the way she'd been flirting all evening? She shivered. He smiled down at her.

'It's cold out here, and there's a wind getting up. Let's go back to my hotel.'

Paula looked into his happy. smiling face and felt awful. The wind whipped back his dark hair. The planes of his face were strong in the moonlight—not a man to cross.

'I'm sorry,' she began.

She felt the arm around her tense until it felt like a steel bar. He looked down at her, and raised both black eyebrows. It was very hard to go on.

'I can't come back with you.'

'Why not?'

Because she'd been living a lie the whole evening, and even now she was too cowardly to admit it.

'I can't tell you.'

He held her close.

'Whatever it is, we'll work through it. You can tell me.'

Paula looked up and met the love and strength and the commitment in his eyes, and she wished with her whole heart that it was her real self who had caused the desire that he so

16

clearly felt for Charlene. All her life she'd longed to be wanted this way, and now when it had happened it was a sham. Emotion choked her.

'I can't. I'm so sorry.'

A single tear rolled down her cheek. Sebastian brushed it away with the pad of one finger, then kissed the place where it had been. He seemed to accept her inability to confide in him. He simply gathered her up and held her close. They stood on the beach together, looking out to the wild sea. All the laughter and warmth of the magical evening seemed to drain away. Paula felt chilled and desolate. Sebastian's face was grim when he looked at her, but his voice was matter-of-fact.

'It's freezing out here. Let's get you back.'

They turned towards Paula's hotel, walking without words, the wind whipping their hair. She could taste salt on her lips and feel goosebumps all down her arm. She shivered again, wishing he'd say something, but he was silent until they arrived back at the hotel. Then he turned and looked down at her gravely. She heard a shake in his voice, and realised with surprise that he was nervous.

'This problem of yours, there wouldn't be a husband or boyfriend waiting for you, by any chance?'

'Oh, no! My goodness, no! What kind of a person do you think I am?'

The words popped out before Paula

remembered what kind of a person she'd been pretending to be all day. She wanted to tell him the truth, to explain why she'd led him on to believe she was different, but when she looked at his face, she saw that he had no intention of pushing her further. He was laughing and his eyes were relieved.

'Great! I'd hate to fall for a married woman!'

'Never married, not even involved,' Paula said truthfully.

Her heart leaped. He'd said he was falling for her. Had he meant it? She checked his face.

His eyes were loving as he said softly, 'Have breakfast with me tomorrow.'

'Where are you staying?'

'Hotel Cutlass. The breakfast bar opens at six.'

Paula almost sang the words, she was so happy.

'I'll be there.'

CHAPTER THREE

Getting to the Hotel Cutlass the next morning wasn't so simple, however. Paula stood in the cold marble lobby of her hotel, looking up at the man who barred her way.

'But I've arranged to meet a friend for

breakfast.'

He lifted a huge hand.

'Our guests cannot leave the hotel during a hurricane warning. It's against safety procedures.'

Paula looked at the transformed world outside. Rain battered at the sliding doors of the lobby. It looked as if the glass panels were being dowsed by a fire hose. Storm clouds streaked across the black sky, and the wet palm trees were bent nearly double by the wind that howled through them. It did look wild. The guard seized his opportunity.

'Please, madam, your friend will understand. You must have breakfast here. The restaurant is opening now.'

Paula could smell coffee and relented, even though she was yearning to see Sebastian again. She'd spent the most ridiculous night, one minute smiling and hugging herself with glee, because she'd met the most wonderful man in the world and he liked her, the next rolling across the white sheets because she seemed so lonely without him. She'd been such a fool to lie to him. She was in too deep to ever explain the truth. It was awful. But it was wonderful, because she'd never had such a marvellous evening.

Even now, she shivered in joy at the memory as she poured herself a cup of coffee and took a seat on a wicker sofa, choosing a table well away from the wild weather so visible out of the big windows. All around her she could hear people complaining. They wanted sunshine and blue skies, and they wanted the hotel to arrange it right now. They want the impossible, Paula thought, and then she sighed, because so did she. She wanted Sebastian and she wanted him now.

'Excuse me, madam.'

Paula recognised the voice of the hotel doorkeeper again, and looked up without much interest. Then she saw a tall figure behind him, a tall, handsome figure with wet, wind-blown black hair and a warm sweater over his shorts. Her coffee cup crashed to the ground and splintered on the marble floor as she leaped to her feet and charged past the guard, flinging herself at Sebastian's strong chest and twining her arms around him.

She held him and kissed him and hugged him even tighter and she was laughing and, for some silly reason, crying as well. Sebastian lifted her off her feet and swung her round. The guard shook his head at them both.

'Well, sir, I guess you found your fiancée OK. Don't leave the hotel without telling me, man, because I have your name on my evacuation list.'

The world seemed to tilt and whirl around Paula. Startled, she looked directly into Sebastian's blue eyes and said to him blankly, 'Fiancée?'

He scooped her into his arms with all the

right of conquest.

'Which is your table?'

Paula revelled in the feeling of being held in his arms before nodding over at where she'd been sitting. Sebastian carried her over and deposited her on the sofa. Then he tipped the maid who was clearing the smashed coffee cup, before snuggling down in the cushions beside her. He kissed the end of her nose.

'We had a date.'

Paula wound her arms around his neck.

'They told me to stay in because of this storm. Coming to find me could have been risky. It looks dangerous out there.'

His eyes were dark and serious.

'All the more reason to be with you. They wouldn't let me go until I told them you were my fiancée and then I realised that I wanted that to be true. I wanted to be with you and to have the right to protect you.'

Her breath caught, and as she returned his gaze she felt her heart thumping. He looked so loving, so determined and so tender as he examined every inch of her face.

'Am I being a fool?' he asked her softly.

It was easy to be honest.

'I was awake most of the night,' she replied.

'Thinking about me?'

Paula looked down, letting her lashes shield the vulnerability she felt in her heart. Her voice was just a whisper.

'Do you think we're crazy?' she answered.

His answer was strong as he held her and said, 'No. We're romantic.'

Her sigh was a surrender, but even as she clung to him physically, she knew her own limits. She drew away from him slightly.

'An affair? Is that what you're suggesting? A wild, bittersweet fling?'

'Aren't you listening to me? I love you. I'm proposing.'

'To me?'

The look in his eyes was ecstasy.

'Yes, Charlene, to you! I've never felt like this before, and I never will. I'll never love anyone else. Marry me and we'll call this our honeymoon.'

The temptation was strong, so strong that it swept Paula away into a whirling state of madness. She'd known this man for less than twenty-four hours. It could take her a week to decide on black shoes or navy! She was never impulsive. She believed whole-heartedly in the old adage, marry in haste, repent at leisure but she flung herself into his arms and lifted her head to meet the love in his blue eyes.

'I'd love to marry you. I love you, too.'

His cry of triumph stopped the noise of the restaurant dead. The place had filled up while they'd been talking. A sea of faces turned towards them, butter knives, breakfast spoons and coffee cups suspended in mid-air. Sebastian's laugh was carefree.

'She's going to marry me!'

The hotel guests laughed. A few of them cheered and banged on the tables. Paula felt surrounded by love, laughter and happiness. The maid who'd cleared up her spilled coffee came back and scolded them.

'You need to give your man breakfast now. Look. he don't even have a drink inside him. What kind of wife are you going to be?'

Wife! The word gave Paula such a shock that she recklessly ordered a banana split for breakfast. Sebastian refused to join her and asked for toast.

'Is this real? Will you truly be mine?' he asked.

'I'll marry you,' she promised him. 'It feels like a dream, but it's real.'

The rest of the day passed in a similar mixture of crazy reality and dreamlike feelings. Paula remembered talking and laughing, playing tennis and swimming in the hotel pool. The weather improved, and at midday the hotel announced that the hurricane had moved harmlessly out to sea, and the guests were free to leave the hotel. Sebastian and Paula spent the rest of the afternoon together. He only left her to make a few phone calls. His face was grim when he came back from the last one.

'I'll have to go into town tomorrow with our passports. The magistrate wants to see me in person before she'll issue the licence.'

'I'll come with you.'

He kissed her and looked at her with warm

23

eyes.

'Don't you need to go shopping?'

'What for?'

'Oh, a dress, flowers, a church. I'll try to get back and help you, but I don't know how long it will take to get the special licence.'

Paula looked at the rose-covered arbour. Despite the flying clouds and still strong breeze, another couple was getting married under the pink blossoms.

'Couldn't we get married at the hotel? It's pretty here.'

'I asked about that, but they're booked up for months. The hotel manager suggested we try the church by the harbour. Let's go now.'

The white-painted church was empty when they got there. The harbour was sheltered from the winds that still blew over the open beach. Bees hummed in and out of the brilliant magenta bougainvillea that tumbled over the walls. Butterflies hovered in the scented air. Paula tilted her head to look up at the white tower. Two silver bells gleamed in the sunshine.

'This is not a real church. It looks like something from a fairy tale. We couldn't possibly get married here.'

'And why not?' a deep, jolly voice inquired behind them.

Paula whirled, and then smiled at the merry giant of a man who stood behind her. He wore a brightly-coloured caftan and love for his

24

fellow man beamed out of his soft brown eyes. Sebastian moved forward and shook the man's hand.

'Are you Reverend Zachariah?'

'That is me, man. And you must be the crazy English couple who met yesterday and now want to get married.'

Paula couldn't believe it.

'How do you know that?'

Reverend Zachariah gave a booming laugh.

'You two are rapidly becoming an island legend. But come in. Marriage is a serious business and I need to talk with you.'

He took them around the side of the church to his house and ushered them into a plain, cool room, where he talked to them very movingly about the importance of marriage. Paula felt tears in her eyes as he spoke, but they were happy tears of pure emotion. Sebastian turned his head towards her and he smiled as he took her hand.

'I agree with every word you've said, sir. I want to get married because it is such a serious commitment. This may have been love at first sight, but it's true love, I'm convinced of it. I want to be with Charlene for ever.'

Paula looked down at the strong fingers clasped around hers, and she felt his steadiness, his commitment, his inner strength. She looked up and spoke tenderly.

'Through good times and bad.'

Reverend Zachariah had been watching

them intently. Now he jumped to his feet, robes billowing, and laughed out loud.

'Good! Good! Let us have some lemonade to celebrate.'

'Then you'll marry us, sir?'

'I cannot say no. I can see that you two love one another, and my heart tells me that this wedding was meant to be.'

He poured three glasses of fresh, tart lemon juice. Then he whipped out an electronic organiser from the folds of his robe. He frowned over it for a moment and then looked up smiling.

'How does ten in the morning on the day after tomorrow sound?'

'Perfect. Thank you, sir.'

'No problem, man. I just love marrying people. Let me have your full names now.'

Paula swallowed nervously and cast a quick look at Sebastian before speaking.

'Paula Elizabeth Jackson.'

She waited for him to explode, but instead he gave her a relieved grin.

'Michael Edward Kent.'

She couldn't stop the laugh that rose in her throat.

'Michael?'

He faced her with an answering smile.

'Paula?'

They exploded with the uninhibited laughter of children who are caught out in innocent naughtiness, and Paula felt such happiness as she watched their delightful minister tapping their names, their true names, into his organiser. Their marriage was going to be perfect.

CHAPTER FOUR

Paula woke up on the morning of her wedding in a cold sweat. She untangled herself from the cotton sheets and padded over the cool marble floor to the balcony. The softness of the early dawn did nothing to reassure her. Every last trace of the hurricane had vanished and the day was splendid and blue, but she felt sick with panic.

She looked at the frothy white wedding dress that hung on the back of the wardrobe door, and felt like kicking it to the ground. No way she was going to look like a meringue and marry a man she'd known only three days, and yesterday didn't count. It had taken him nearly the whole day to cut through the red tape and sort out the licence. How she wished now that he'd failed. She didn't want to marry this stranger.

Paula reached for her wrap, her swimsuit and her sandals. She pulled on the suit, but didn't even pause to wash her face. She just ran out into the cool morning carrying her sandals in one hand. She'd have to see him and

27

explain. It was only fair. She might be going to jilt the man, but she wouldn't leave him at the altar.

The beach was magnificent, fresh, empty, sweet with the promise of a new day. Flocks of little birds ran along the water's edge, making shrill peeping noises as they went. The pale sky arched high above her, and it seemed as if the whole world belonged to her, except for one small figure coming her way. She wasn't surprised as she got closer to the figure to see that she recognised it. With her first sight of him all her doubts melted away. She ran away from him, smiling, but he caught up with her easily, ignoring her squeals of protest.

'Mike! You're not supposed to see me this morning!'

He laughed out loud and hugged her.

'I think we've broken every convention there is to break, don't you?'

'Is it going to be all right?' she asked anxiously.

'Trust me,' was all he said softly, but she could see in his eyes that he was promising so much more, and as she returned to the hotel to get ready, there was nothing in her heart but love and calm purpose.

Standing outside the door of the white church in the hot sun, Paula felt a little sad as she took the arm of Benjamin, Reverend Zachariah's brother, who'd offered to give her away.

'Missing your family?' he asked sympathetically.

'Mum will be sorry to miss my wedding,' she said sadly.

Benjamin gave a deep, rich laugh that sounded just like his brother's.

'You want to change your mind? Wait a little longer?'

Paula looked down at her dress, so beautifully foaming and white. Her fabulous trailing bouquet smelled wonderfully of roses. She thought, too, of how hard everyone had worked to make things happen in time, and she shook her head firmly.

'I'm ready to get married.'

The doors opened and she felt better at once as she heard the wedding march played on steel drums. The rows were packed, and she was amazed to see how many faces she recognised. The hairdresser, the hotel staff, the woman who'd sold her the gold wedding rings, the nice people she'd talked to on the plane, the hotel guests—they had all come to wish her well.

The lonely feeling in her heart subsided, and when she saw Mike in a morning suit, looking at once proud and nervous as he waited with his best man by the altar, all her doubts vanished to be replaced by a glorious certainty. The ceremony was short, but moving. Reverend Zachariah preached a lovely sermon on the blessings of love. They were pelted with showers of rose petals and confetti. A reporter from the local paper interviewed them both, and the photographers promised to send copies of all the photographs to England. She was married.

'Alone at last, Mrs Kent,' Michael said, much later, back in their hotel room, kissing her lovingly.

'I'm glad your name isn't really Sebastian,' Paula murmured. 'Mike is much nicer.'

She twisted around in his arms so that she could look up at his face.

'I don't know anything about you! I don't know what you do, where you live, where you went to school, not even what your star sign is.'

Mike's blue eyes were steady and loving.

'We have the rest of our lives to find out. Won't that be fun?'

'It will be, because I love you,' she said simply.

He reached for her but she pulled away.

'Just a minute!'

'What?'

Paula laughed and held out the **Do Not Disturb** sign.

'Hadn't we better put this on the door?'

Mike let her go so that she could hang the sign, but then he said huskily, 'Come here, wife, and quit delaying.'

Paula screamed as he swept her up in his arms and threw her on to the bed, but he lay beside her gently and framed her face in his

30

hands.

'I'll never hurt you,' he promised.

Just before dawn, Paula woke early, luxuriating in the warmth from the heat of his body. She stretched sensuously on the white cotton sheet and looked out at the pale, morning sky. Hibiscus grew in pots on the balcony, and a humming bird flashed past and paused briefly to sip at the nectar. She turned to look at Mike's sleeping face.

This is happiness, she thought in wonder, as he woke and reached for her sleepily. This is love and I've found it. I'm happy at last.

The rest of their honeymoon was perfect. The holiday company reps even managed to switch seats on the coach for them, so that they could travel to the airport together. As they waited in line at the check-in, Paula looked at Mike curiously.

'How did you manage to get me on your plane?'

She saw a gleam of pride in his eyes, and knew he was pleased that she'd asked.

'Remember my best man? I convinced him that he'd much rather travel home on your plane than back with me.'

'The best man is our friend? But we never saw him again after the wedding!'

Mike's tone was possessive.

'I didn't want him hanging about on my honeymoon. Besides, he made lots of new friends.'

31

'You heartless beast!'

'Maybe, but I'm good at arranging things. It wasn't easy to get the seats changed. The airlines don't usually allow it.'

A man and a woman in the uniform of the airline approached them, carrying champagne.

'But we're suckers for a romantic story,' the woman said, smiling.

'Compliments of the captain,' the man said, handing over the champagne. 'How would you like to fly home? First class?'

Paula did try to talk seriously to Mike on the way home, but what with champagne and congratulations there never seemed to be an opening.

'Let's not watch the movie,' she suggested. 'I want to talk to you. You need to know. I'm not—'

He stopped her words with a fingertip and a champagne kiss.

'Don't look so serious. We'll get to know each other all in good time.'

Paula wondered if she should insist, but a flight attendant barged in between them. By the time the woman had given them a saucer heaped with complimentary truffles the moment had passed.

Mike gave her a reassuring hug and whispered, 'Wait till we get home.'

Paula snuggled into his shoulder and made up her mind to enjoy the film. Later, their first-class seats were made into amazingly comfortable beds. She and Mike fell asleep holding hands. It was hard to wake up in the morning, or was it night? Paula stood shivering on the dark Tarmac of Manchester airport.

'I can't believe how cold the air is! What time is it?'

'Ten o'clock at night, I think.'

A brightly-lit bus trundled towards them. It didn't feel much warmer inside the bus. They passed smoothly through customs and were through the formalities in no time. Paula looked at the stranger beside her.

'Do you mind if I ask you a question, new husband?'

'Ask away,' he said cheerfully, heading towards the taxi rank.

'Where are we going to live, and even more importantly, where are we going to spend the night?'

'Good question,' he said cheerfully. 'Do you want to go to your place?'

When she met the love in his eyes it was hard to worry about anything.

'I only have a single bed.'

'My place then. I have a double.'

'But I have to be at work for nine o'clock.'

'Then we'll take a taxi to your place, get all you need for the morning, and hurry home to my double bed.'

They kissed in the taxi all the way to Paula's. Mike was wide-eyed when he saw her immaculate minimalist decor.

'Wow! And I thought I was tidy!'

Paula had left the heating on low, but her place felt cold and somehow forlorn. It seemed strange to open her wardrobe and take out a familiar grey suit for work. So much had happened since she had last worn it. She hesitated over the flashing light on her answer machine.

'The taxi will wait if you want to take your messages,' Mike said.

'No. I'm feeling tired now, and if I talk to anyone I'll have to tell them the news, and that will take all night.'

'The good news!' Mike corrected, picking up her suitcase.

The very good news, Paula thought on their way to Mike's place.

'Newly-weds, huh?' the cabby said.

'You got that right!' Mike laughed, tipping him.

Paula tried to pick up one of the suitcases, but Mike wouldn't let her.

'Stand still a moment while I switch off the burglar alarm.'

Paula waited obediently on the path, shivering in the night air. She was taken by surprise when Mike returned with a swoop and swept her up in his arms to carry her through the door and into his front room.

'It is traditional, you know,' he told her, laughing.

Paula felt breathless as she kissed him.

'We've been married for three days now, and we spent last night apart. Come to bed, wife!'

'We slept on the plane!'

Paula protested, but she didn't protest too much. She felt dizzy with love and with tiredness, and surely jetlag was affecting her, too, because she collapsed into his arms with unaccustomed meekness. She barely had time to examine Mike's house. She did notice that it was new, and she formed an impression of space, and, as promised, tidiness, as he swept her into his arms and carried her upstairs.

She still felt disorientated the next morning as they breakfasted together in Mike's neat kitchen. He was in a smart navy suit and crisp white shirt.

'You look very high-powered,' she said nervously.

'I am,' he told her, laughing.

'This is a strange question to ask one's husband, but what do you do?' A slightly-evasive look sprang to his eyes before he answered.

'I'm the finance director for a factory with a billion-pound turnover. Now, let me ask my wife the same question. What do you do?'

Paula swallowed nervously.

'I'm an accountant.'

She felt Mike's gaze sweep over her grey suit, her white blouse and neatly-plaited hair. She might as well admit the whole truth now.

She rummaged in the black bag that matched her black shoes.

'And I can't see much without my glasses. I was only pretending to be glamorous. Are you disappointed?'

She perched her glasses on her nose and looked at Mike apprehensively, but he laughed out loud and held out his arms to her. His eyes were warm.

'Charlene didn't fool me for long, angel. I might have been game for a holiday fling with a wild siren, but that's as far as it would have gone. I married the real you, the woman that looks out of your eyes, sweet, honest, gentle, true.'

Paula jumped up from her seat and flew into his open arms. She felt a rush of happiness so pure that she wanted to cry, but her confessions were not quite over yet. Her words were muffled as she spoke into his tie.

'There's more.'

He tilted her head back so that he could see her face. His expression encouraged her to go on.

'Everyone laughs when they hear where I work.'

He made a startled movement, as if he was going to say something, but then he seemed to change his mind and wait for her to finish first.

'You can tell me, sweetheart.'

'Well, I work for a sausage factory. Mackenzie's Sausages, to be exact.'

His body stiffened as if someone had hit him a mighty blow, but he didn't laugh. Paula looked up at his face nervously. His cheeks were white under his tan and there was a stunned expression in his eyes. Was he so horrified to find out that his wife worked in such an absurd profession?

'Most people find sausages funny,' she probed gently.

Mike's arms unwrapped themselves from her body and he tottered backwards and fell limply into a kitchen chair.

'Mike, what's wrong? Please tell me.'

His expression was stricken as he lifted his head to meet her eyes.

'I work for Sizzling Sausages.'

Paula's mind whirled. Mike was in the same trade as she was! But the news was no relief to her overwrought nerves. The Mackenzie brothers had started out in business together until a bitter quarrel, whose origin no-one could even remember, split them apart. The two men were now deadly rivals. They weren't just in competition in the same market, it was combat on the commercial field. And the first rule of that war was no fraternisation with the enemy.

'This is awful!' she gasped in disbelief.

Mike ran a hand through his hair, and even in her confusion she longed to smooth down the shining strands, and there was nothing to stop her. She reached out and touched his hair gently as she amended her words.

'Not our marriage, of course, but the situation. Why didn't you tell me?'

'Why didn't you tell me?' Mike countered, but he took hold of her hand and turned it over, kissing the wrist.

'It's kind of funny, really,' she said softly.

Mike had seen the watch that she wore on the wrist that he was kissing.

'Not as funny as unemployment will be. Look at the time!'

'What are we going to do?'

His brow furrowed for a moment and then cleared. He went to a drawer and came back with a spare key and two leather bootlaces.

'We're going to be late if we don't leave now.'

But he took his time about whispering the alarm combination to his house into her ear. Paula twisted away from his kisses, laughing.

'That tickles!'

His eyes were alight with laughter.

'Deliciously, I hope.'

And then his eyes turned serious. He took off his wedding ring and slipped it gently on to one of the leather laces, tying it around his neck. His words were a promise.

'I'm never going to be parted from my ring.'

Paula let him slide the gold band off her third finger.

'Nor me,' she vowed softly.

Their eyes met in a look of loving promise

as he slipped the lace over her neck. And then they both looked at the kitchen clock and screamed.

'I'll take you to the bus stop. Tell no-one our secret today. Do you know the Spanish Tapas bar in town? Meet me there after work, and we'll make a plan. But remember, tell no-one! Our marriage must stay a secret from our employers for the moment.'

CHAPTER FIVE

All through the long morning that followed, Paula sat at her familiar desk in her familiar office and kept reaching up to touch her ring. By ten o'clock, she decided she'd gone mad and imagined the whole strange business of her marriage. She slipped into the ladies and drew the gold circle out from under her blouse. It was real, and so was Mike.

The door clicked behind her and she hastily hid the simple gold hoop.

'Hello, Paula,' her colleague said. 'You look as if you had a good holiday. How was the Caribbean?'

Wild! Wonderful! Romantic, Paula thought, but before she could frame a conventional remark about the hotel being nice, her colleague had started to tell her all about her last, terrible holiday in Spain.

'So Jim said you could put him in a coffin before he'd go abroad again, and I can't say I blame him. That reminds me. Mr Mackenzie was shouting for you earlier.'

Paula scuttled down the familiar grey corridor that led to her boss's office, feeling as if she was in a dream. The factory couldn't have changed physically in a week, so it must be her who was different, but as she knocked on the panels of the gleaming, wooden door she felt as if she'd never been in Mr Mackenzie's office in her life before. It was difficult to concentrate on the scene that was taking place inside. Her peppery little boss was bouncing up and down behind his desk.

'I say that we sue him. I won't stand for industrial espionage.'

The finance director, James Cole, shifted his weight from one foot to the other and cleared his throat before speaking.

'The outcome of such cases can never be predicted with certainty.'

Rory Mackenzie's eyes bulged.

'Certainty! I'm certain enough that he stole my Spicy Thai Sausage recipe. It's a clear-cut case of stealing, and I won't stand for it. Sue him.'

'Oh, well, if you say so, sir.'

Paula watched Rory Mackenzie steamrollering his way over the finance director and just couldn't get interested. She was in the middle of picturing kissing Mike on a Caribbean beach when Rory turned to her.

'What do you say, girl?' he barked out.

It wasn't always easy to tell her boss something he didn't want to hear. Paula had always tried to tell the truth in the past, but she'd never opposed him with the carefree nonchalance that she displayed now.

'It's madness to sue.'

Rory's bristly eyebrows flew upwards like two furry caterpillars.

'What? Why's that, girl? What makes you say that?'

'Paula, my name's Paula,' she reminded him patiently. 'I don't think we should get involved in any more court cases.'

The finance director looked down his nose at her.

'I hardly think it's your position to make that kind of decision.'

Instead of feeling crushed, Paula merely shrugged.

'Mr Mackenzie asked me what I thought, so I told him, that's all.'

An uneasy silence fell. James Cole couldn't have looked more surprised and Rory Mackenzie was breathing hard. His eyebrows twitched again.

'Explain!' he bawled out finally.

Paula was amazed how calm and unconcerned her voice sounded.

'Part of my job is to minimise expenses. Last year we spent an incredible twenty per cent of our profits on litigation. I couldn't possibly recommend spending any more, especially as we usually lose.'

'Those nitwit judges don't take sausages seriously,' Rory exploded, with real feeling. 'They'd find in our favour fast enough if I ran a nuclear power plant here, oh, yes. They'd be quick enough to take us seriously then. I don't know where they get these judges from. Last one was smirking all over his face at us. My best recipe stolen by those scoundrels at Sizzling Sausages and he thought it was funny! There's nothing funny about industrial espionage, nothing at all.'

A brooding silence fell. The finance director cleared this throat.

'Shall I instruct our lawyers?'

Rory Mackenzie sat up and waved a plump hand.

'No, no. The girl's right. We'll probably end up in court as it is. Last I saw of the culprit, he was threatening to sue me for unfair dismissal. I'm not afraid to go to court, I told him. You just try telling the judge what you were doing in the carpark of Sizzling Sausages, I said. Try getting out of that one.'

Paula's heart sank inside her as she faced her peppery employer.

'You must have had more reason than that to sack the man.'

'Reason? Don't you think slinking around our main competitor is reason enough to fire a man? Hey? I'd call it good reason.'

Paula closed her eyes and felt faint. The plan of action she'd been formulating blew away like smoke. Confiding the truth about her marriage to Mr Mackenzie and throwing herself on his mercy was not going to work at present. She opened her eyes again.

'It sounds like rampant paranoia to me.'

James Cole sucked in his breath sharply.

'Miss Jackson! How dare you!'

Mrs Kent was completely unmoved by the finance director's reprimand. Rory Mackenzie regarded her with hot, angry eyes, but Paula faced him calmly. Being sacked would be one way of solving her problems! But to her amazement she saw the anger clear away like a summer storm and her boss's hazel eyes started to twinkle. He even gave a rusty chuckle.

'I like a woman who's not afraid to stand up to me! Yes, I do. I like your style, girl, but you're completely wrong. I won't sue, but I will continue to sack anyone found fraternising with the enemy. It's in all the contracts. No fraternising. It's written in. You all know that!'

His good humour was a complete surprise to Paula. The last time she'd disagreed with him, he'd thrown his silver-plated inkstand at her. She couldn't understand why his expression was so benevolent today. In fact, the man looked as merry as a cherub as he sent the toadying James away. He even

43

attempted a joke.

'Now then, my dear, sit down. I might chew your ears off, but I won't eat you. Would you like a drink?'

Too bemused to refuse, Paula found herself accepting a cup of coffee in the company's best china. She watched her boss warily as he fussed with the items on his desk. Should she put in her notice? It might be nice to leave and find an employer with a shorter fuse. On the other hand, she'd worked for the company since she left school. It would be difficult to find another business that would trust a female as young as she was with an equally responsible position. She'd wait and see what Mike suggested that evening. She regarded the volatile sausage maker and wondered what was coming. His expression was unreadable.

'Do you know my son, Nigel?' he said suddenly.

'No. I've never met him.'

'He's a good boy is my Nigel, yes, he is and he'll make a fine husband one of these days, when he gets this madness out of his system.'

'Madness?' Paula asked cautiously.

'Aye, madness. Modern art, he calls it. Wasting good materials and my time and money I call it, and I've had enough. I've told him I'm not paying no more of those bills just so he can play around with a lot of junk. He's got his degree now and that's where it stops. I can't be keeping him for ever.'

Paula kept quiet and nodded sympathetically.

'His mother thinks he'll be famous one day, but that's women all over for you. I keep telling her she's soft and all she does is laugh at me. But anyway, it's Nigel I want to talk to you about. He's back from Paris, you see, and he can't be spending all his time with his old parents. You're a nice, steady girl with a good head on your shoulders. Have dinner with him on Saturday night. I know you're single. At least, you were last week. Don't suppose you're the type to have one of those holiday romances, hey?'

It was all Paula could do not to fall off her chair. What mad plan was her boss hatching?

'I'm sorry . . .' she began, groping for an excuse.

But her poor, surprised brain was stunned into silence and she couldn't finish her sentence. She sat groping for plausible reasons to escape the proposed date, while Rory Mackenzie leaned forward, looking pleased.

'That's settled then. I'll book you a table at the Royal Albert Restaurant. Nice, plain cooking they do there. Seven o'clock suit you?'

Paula was feeling too desperate to be tactful.

'You can't arrange your son's Saturday night without consulting him!'

Her boss gave her a blank stare.

'Can't I?'

Paula understood completely why Rory's son had needed to go to Paris to study. Arguing with his father would be like trying to stop a juggernaut. Obviously considering the conversation at an end, Rory Mackenzie got to his feet and walked across the office to open the door. Paula stood up and realised that her knees were shaking. She hunted for an argument to change her boss's mind, but all she could find was a slender straw.

'I'm much older than Nigel.'

A beaming smile spread across Rory Mackenzie's cherubic countenance as he put a hand under Paula's elbow.

'Just what the lad needs. A wife with a bit of commonsense who's old enough to know what's what.'

The office door closed firmly behind her. Paula stared blankly at the beaming wooden panels. Her lips framed just the one word.

'Wife!'

'Wife!' she repeated again that evening as she made her way along the wet grey Manchester street where the Tapas Bar was. She shivered and hunched her shoulders against the February cold, walking fast because she wanted to be out of the biting wind. As she pushed open the door into the brightly-lit interior of the bar, there was Mike. He came to meet her at once, his eyes alight with love.

The bar was small, noisy and crowded. It was also lovely and warm and she took off her

46

coat and sank gratefully into the seat at the table for two that Mike had found for them. A busy waiter plonked plates of glistening black and green olives in herbs on the table, rapidly followed by an anchovy salad, wedges of Spanish omelette and a dish of salt potatoes.

'I didn't know what you'd want so I ordered everything,' Mike explained.

That holiday feeling was returning. How nice to be sitting in a glamorous bar with a handsome man instead of going home alone to a warmed-up meal for one! Paula regarded the generous quantities of food on the table and felt her difficult day melt away.

'Oh, Mike, I do love you.'

His blue eyes blazed, and then dimmed.

'And I you, but Paula, you'll never believe the day I've had.'

'I think I can top it,' she said ruefully, but Mike wasn't listening.

'Old Mackenzie wants me to go to the Royal Albert Hotel on Saturday night.'

'That's so weird, such a coincidence! I have to go there, too! Do you have a business meeting?'

Mike looked uncomfortable.

'Look, Paula, this might be difficult to understand, but when old Mackenzie issues an order, it's by way of being a royal command.'

'I work for a Mackenzie, too,' she reminded him.

'Yes, but this is so odd I don't know if you'll

believe me.'

Paula stopped eating and gazed at him with her fork in mid-air.

'What?'

He drew in a deep breath and then let it out rapidly.

'Well, old Mackenzie's daughter appears to be a bit of a rebel. She's been living on a ranch in Argentina, horse mad, they say. Well, she's home now, and I've been told to take Georgina out for dinner on Saturday night.'

When Paula simply stared at him, he looked worried and reached for both of her hands.

'Paula, don't look like that, please. It's not what you're thinking. I've never even met the girl, but Mackenzie knew I was single before I went away and I can't tell him that in a week I've met and married a woman who works for his sworn enemy. He caught me by surprise. I couldn't think of a way to get out of it. Do you believe me? Oh, Paula, say you believe me.'

'I believe you,' she said slowly. 'I suppose he's decided that it's time his daughter stopped running wild and what she needs is to meet a nice, steady man with a sound, financial head on his shoulders.'

Mike's jaw dropped.

'Suffering cats! Have you got our office bugged?'

Paula didn't know whether she felt more like laughing or crying.

'The Mackenzies are brothers, after all. I

guess their minds must work the same way. Didn't you hear me say I had to go to the restaurant at the Royal Albert Hotel on Saturday night, too?'

'Isn't it a business meeting?'

'Rory Mackenzie's son has been painting in Paris, and his father thinks it's time he stopped.'

Mike nearly leaped out of his seat.

'You're not going on a date!'

'No more than you are.'

'That's different. I have to go.'

Paula gave him a sunny smile.

'So do I.'

'I'm not having my wife running around with strange men.'

'Mike, let's be reasonable. I have to go just as much as you do. I need to keep my job.'

Jealousy fizzed in his eyes.

'No, you don't. I'll look after you. You let the old codger find someone else for his son.'

Mike grasped her hands tightly, and his eyes were very earnest.

'I'm serious. You're my wife and I'm proud of you. I hate keeping quiet about our marriage. Leave your job and I can shout it from the rooftops.'

Paula was tempted. It was so nice to have a man care about her. Who didn't want to be looked after? But then her sense of independence reasserted itself.

'You leave your job,' she suggested. 'I'll look

49

after you.'

'Get real!'

His immediate dismissal of her offer caught Paula on the raw.

'We could live on my salary,' she suggested.

Mike dismissed her offer with a terse comment.

'Could you pay the mortgage on my house?'

Paula looked around at the crowds of happy, chattering people. They all looked so light-hearted. She suddenly wished she and Mike weren't having this serious conversation, but it was important.

'I couldn't but you could live with me.'

Mike's look of scorn made her feel awful.

'Your place is tiny. You don't even have a double bed.'

'Size isn't everything,' she managed to mutter, but her attempt at a joke didn't make her feel any better about the way he'd reacted.

Mike looked horrified when he saw that tears were welling in her eyes.

'Darling, let's not argue.'

'But we do need to talk.'

'Of course we do, and I didn't mean to upset you, Paula. But we can't both lose our jobs and as I'm older than you and higher up the ladder than you are, it makes more sense for you to leave. I can easily support us both.'

Pain stabbed at Paula's heart, and it made her feel stubborn. She'd worked so hard to get where she was, but it was clear that Mike didn't value her achievements because he was suggesting she throw everything away.

'I'm not about to sacrifice my career.'

'Nobody's asking you to,' Mike replied. 'You can get a little job if you want to work.'

Paula didn't like the note of superiority she caught in his tone. She looked into his lovely blue eyes and realised she knew nothing about him.

'Mike! What have we done?'

His answer belonged to the man she'd met in the Caribbean sunshine.

'We've fallen in love, that's all.'

'That was unreal. This is reality, finding out that we know nothing about one another.'

He reached out and touched her face gently.

'It's a real fairy-tale romance. I know that.'

She wanted to throw herself into his arms. She felt like a drowning woman as she met the love in his eyes, but still she kept fighting.

'Can love survive in the real world?'

His words were a promise.

'All fairy tales have happy endings. You just follow the rules. The princess moves into the prince's castle and they live happily ever after.'

Paula wished life was so simple. She looked pleadingly into his face.

'Tell me we haven't made a terrible mistake.'

His blue eyes were very dark and soft in the dim light of the bar. His gaze examined her face carefully, and he seemed satisfied with what he saw there. His voice was very gentle, and lulled her as he wove his magic spell.

'We've been home for exactly one day! It takes most people a year, or even two to get married. We're doing it backwards, that's all. Marriage first, arrangements later. Of course it's going to take time to sort out all the details, but does any of it matter when we love each other so much?'

There was only one answer to that.

'Oh, Mike, darling!'

He kissed her lips gently, and at the first touch she was filled with all the energy and excitement of their love.

'Our first kiss and make-up,' he murmured.

Careless of the bar full of people, Paula leaned closer across the table so that he could wind his arms around her and she could nestle into his arms and kiss him properly. The bustle of an English pub faded away, the noise of the conversations around them seemed to change into the sound of pounding surf. Hot, tropical air seemed to shimmer around them as they kissed. An age later, Paula pulled away and looked up at her husband dreamily.

'Oh, Mike, what are we going to do?'

She found that she hardly cared about the answer as Mike looked at her with smiling eyes.

'Until we come up with a plan, we'll just have to go on with the deception, including our dates on Saturday. At least we'll be able to keep an eye on each other! Those Mackenzie brothers have no imagination at all. Fancy sending us to the same restaurant!'

'It seems strange that the families never speak. What did they argue about? Do you know?'

Mike shook his head. A waiter cleared their plates and asked them if they wanted another drink.

'No, thank you,' Mike said, and then he smiled at Paula.

'There's not much in the house. Shall we go shopping together before we go home?'

Shopping together, how lovely that sounded. Paula pushed aside the issues they'd left unresolved and lost herself in the delight of having a man to help her on with her coat, usher her tenderly across the road, and seat her in his nice, warm car. It was fun going around the supermarket together as well. Mike displayed an unexpectedly extravagant streak.

'You can't have steak and salmon and prawns and roast beef in one week!' Paula admonished him.

She loved the way his eyes lit up when he laughed.

'And why not?'

'Well, I usually have something cheaper during the week. You can splash out at weekends.'

He threw back his head, laughed out loud and thumped his chest.

'But, darling, you've got a husband to feed you now. Me big successful hunter! Me get good meat for my woman.'

'Mike! For goodness' sake! Everyone's looking at you! Oh, don't make me laugh. Mike, you can't kiss me here. Mike! Oh, no! Stop. I'm serious. You really must stop. Here comes the biggest gossip in Manchester. Don't say a word! Let me talk to her. Hello, Mrs Meldrew.'

Mrs Meldrew zoomed down the aisle and screeched to a halt next to them, looking at Mike curiously. The nosey neighbour folded her arms across the top of the trolley handle and settled in for a good gossip.

'Hello, Paula. Who's the new boyfriend?'

Mike gave the bleached and overdone woman an incredulous look and turned away. From the corner of one eye, Paula saw that he was pretending to study cuts of meat in the chilled cabinet, but she was also aware that his shoulders were shaking and she heard him mutter, 'Does she always go straight for the jugular?'

Paula summoned up her best smile.

'Not a boyfriend, Mrs Meldrew.'

'Really? You'll have to introduce me, and our Gail. She's out shopping with me today, you know. She's a lovely girl is our Gail.'

Our Gail had spotted a good-looking man. She cantered down the aisle to join them. She looked just like her mother and smelled like she was wearing every free perfume sample she'd ever been given. Mike seemed to have got himself under control. At least, he took his face out of the meat cabinet and turned around so that Paula could introduce him.

'This is my friend, Sebastian,' she said.

Mike shook hands and smiled charmingly. Two female hearts were won at once. Mrs Meldrew gave him a flirtatious smile.

'You look ever so brown, too. You didn't go away with Paula, did you?'

'We were at the same resort, as it happens,' Mike said truthfully. 'But I went on holiday with a friend from work.'

Gail looked from Mike's face to Paula's. She was as blunt as her mother.

'You're not an item then?'

Paula saw a deep, and utterly charming dimple appear at the corner of Mike's mouth, but he managed not to laugh. Then she was struggling with her own laughter as he answered with a completely straight face.

'I don't think one could forge much of a meaningful relationship in a week, do you Gail?'

Gail flushed and fluttered her lashes. Then, to Paula's amazed fury, right there in the supermarket aisle, Gail wriggled her chest at Mike.

Get your hands off my husband, Paula thought angrily. And then she was astonished, because she'd never known that she was the jealous type. She was though! As she watched Gail posing and touching her bleached hair, she realised how much she disliked the girl, a feeling that intensified as she took in what she was saying.

'I should have known that a whirlwind romance wouldn't be Paula's style. I wish I could be as cool as she is. I envy her that practical streak, but I'm the kind of person who feels things very deeply, you know, Sebastian. I'm sensitive. I can't help it, it's just the way I am. I could never be hard-nosed.'

Paula was filled with the deepest feeling she'd ever had—a fervent desire to throttle Gail Meldrew! Mike had had enough, too. He gave both women a perfectly delightful smile, but there was an authority in his voice and actions that made them fall back.

'What a pity that I live in Glasgow, Gail, as we'll never meet again. You'll have to excuse me. I'm here to visit a friend in hospital and it would never do to miss visiting hours.'

It took all Paula's willpower not to be impressed by his masterful manner as he swept her away towards the grocery section, saying disdainfully, 'What a dreadful pair!'

She laughed a little ruefully.

'Most of the neighbours are lovely. It's a pity you had to meet those two first. Wait a minute, Mike. I want to buy some chocolates for Sally. I'll have to go and see her tonight.'

Mike selected the most delicious box on

display and put it in the trolley, but then he turned to her and said firmly, 'Not tonight.'

'She's my best friend, Mike. She'll think it's strange if I don't call in this evening.'

'You're married now. I want you tonight.'

'I can't tell Sally that.'

'I don't care about Sally.'

'You should do. If she hadn't broken her ankle, we'd never have met.'

'Really?'

Mike steered the trolley towards the rows of gleaming bottles and added a huge bottle of rum to their shopping.

'For Sally,' he announced, 'because she deserves it. We'll buy her some grapes as well.'

'Then you do understand?'

He looked down at her with serious blue eyes. There was a hunger in them that made her feel faint.

'I understand you're a good friend, Paula, but things are different now.'

Her head whirled. If only she was free to hurl herself into his arms and respond to the wild passion that blazed from him, but the very fact that they were having this conversation while standing in an unromantic supermarket aisle helped to remind her that they were back in the real world.

'Very different,' she agreed ruefully. 'We're not free spirits on a tropical island any more. But, Mike, seeing Sally won't take long.'

She turned the trolley towards the fresh

fruit section.

'Jobs, friends, duty, restrictions, chores,' he grumbled. 'There's too much keeping us apart. What else do we need?'

'Clothes for the morning,' Paula said. 'I'll have to go home for those.'

Mike picked out a huge bunch of grapes for Sally, then he added peaches, strawberries and a melon the size of a football to the trolley.

'Come on, then. Let's get it over with. Do you want to go to your flat first or to see this Sally person first?'

Alarmed by the grumble in his tone, Paula examined his face. She was relieved to see that his dimples were showing and his eyes were smiling.

'You don't mind?'

'I won't have to.'

As she stood in the queue at the checkout next to her handsome husband, Paula wished she was free to forget the world and rush off to be alone with him, especially when he stood behind her and put his arms around her in a warm hug. It was so nice to be held, and the top of her head fitted neatly under his chin. She leaned back into his warm embrace.

'I could give Sally a ring and say I'll call round tomorrow.'

Mike laughed.

'Then we'd have exactly the same problem tomorrow! I want you all to myself, Paula, but I know that's not going to happen. Could we go tell her? It would make it easier if she knew the truth.'

Paula shook her head, then regretfully stepped away from Mike because it was their turn to load groceries on to the moving belt.

'I love her to bits, but Sally likes to talk more than she likes to eat! With the best will in the world. she'd never keep a secret.'

'Come on, then,' Mike said, resigned. 'The quicker we get these chores over with the quicker we can go home!'

They went to Paula's tiny apartment first, and this time she packed a big suitcase. Mike nodded approvingly.

'We'll come back at the weekend and pack everything else you need,' he told her. 'Do you want to sell this place or rent it?'

Paula felt dizzy.

'Goodness, I don't know. I haven't had time to think about it.'

His tone was supportive and he hugged her tenderly as he spoke.

'Of course, you haven't. Don't worry, we'll get it sorted out in time.'

She went into his arms with the same feeling of abandon that she'd displayed in the Caribbean. He kissed her, and kissed her again. Paula felt the madness of their love racing through her veins, making her heart beat and her body tingle.

As Mike carried her suitcase down to his car, Paula sat at her kitchen table and flicked the switch on the answer machine. She hardly listened to the messages. They all seemed to belong to a dim and distant world where she hadn't known Mike and she'd never felt love. She did smile when she reached an early message from Sally.

'I know you're away,' the chatty voice gabbled, 'but I just had to tell you this marvellous story.'

Mike came back while the tale was still being told.

'A woman who gossips to an answer machine!'

Paula laughed.

'That's why we can't tell her our secret.'

The next message was from her mother.

'Hello, love,' began the familiar tones.

Paula felt dreadful.

'Oh, Mike. I can't bear the thought of keeping a secret from Mum.'

He touched her hair and then stroked her shoulders with gentle hands.

'What shall we do about our parents? I won't say anything to mine. They are going to go ballistic anyway, so I might as well save up all the news for one colossal row.'

Paula looked at her husband, surprised by the casual way he spoke about his parents. But they had too many problems to deal with in the here and now for her to explore the matter, and his stance made it easier for her to make a decision.

'Then I won't tell mine, either, not until we've worked out a strategy, or one of us has found a new job.'

Mike was listening to something else. He was staring at the answer machine and he looked absolutely horrified.

'Play your mother's message again,' he demanded. 'What was that about your niece?'

Paula hit the replay button and this time paid attention to the meaning of the message. By the end of her mother's words, her head was in her hands and she was groaning.

'It's true! I did offer to have Mandy to stay! But that was before I got married!'

Mike ran both hands through his glossy black hair.

'Tell your family that things have changed.'

'In a week? Besides, I promised.'

Mike's hair stuck up like the spikes of a hedgehog as he ran his hands again and again through the black mass.

'You're at work all day! You can't leave a little girl alone in your flat.'

'She's fifteen, Mike, and studying for exams at school. I won't bore you with the whole story now, but things at my sister's are a bit chaotic, and I promised Mandy that she could always find sanctuary here.'

His eyes were like hard blue chips of sapphire.

'It couldn't be less convenient.'

Paula took in the bleakness of his

expression and realised how little she knew about her new husband. The conflict between her family duties and her desire to be with him was tearing her apart.

'I can't cope!' she said gloomily.

Mike's expression softened.

'Don't worry, darling. We'll think of an excuse not to have her.'

Paula felt as if events were coming at her faster than a freight train and knocking her flat. She hated to argue with him, but Mike's solution didn't feel right.

'I promised her, and Mandy's had too many let-downs in her life as it is. I don't want to add to that list.'

'Isn't this your sister's problem? She is the child's mother, after all.'

'She's not, actually. Mandy was her first husband's child from a previous marriage.'

Mike said slowly, 'He didn't want his own child?'

Paula shook her head.

'And neither did her natural mother.'

His blue eyes were shadowed and serious.

'Poor Mandy. I'm glad your sister took her.'

'Yes, and it worked out fine, except that Clare's getting married again. Peter's really nice, but he's got four children. They're lovely kids, most of the time, but there's Mandy's half brother as well. I must admit that the whole crew's been fighting. I'm sure it will all work out in the end, but Mandy's at a difficult stage and she wants to do well in her exams.'

Mike let out a deep breath and put his arms around her.

'I already know the answer to this, but can't your parents have her?'

'They'd love to, but they live in Cheshire, miles from Mandy's school.'

Paula felt her heart beating a little faster in the pause that followed. She loved him with all her heart, but she knew nothing about Mike's character or his feelings about family duties. How was he going to respond to her dilemma? His face was very serious as he bent forward and kissed her.

'Could we let Mandy in on our secret and have her live with us?'

Paula felt a rush of relief and love which made her want to agree to his suggestion even more, but doubts plagued her.

'I don't know how fair that is, asking Mandy to keep things from her family. She's very young for her age.'

Mike sighed gently and wrapped his arms around her and laid his cheek against hers, seemingly content to just be next to her. Her sixth sense was telling her that he wouldn't argue any more, and she smiled quietly to herself as she waited for him to speak.

'Come on, then, Auntie Paula. Let's make the most of our last night together. You can have ten minutes with your friend, Sally, on the way home. I don't care what excuse you make to her for leaving, but if you're not back in my car in ten minutes, I swear I'll go in and get you and carry you out.'

And then he laughed and looked at her with eyes which held amusement and chagrin.

'I need caveman tactics to get any time alone with you! I'm going to buy a big stick to keep off my rivals!'

Paula's heart was light as she twined her arms around her new husband's neck. She felt his heart beating rapidly as he pulled her close to kiss her, and at the touch of his lips, although nothing had been solved, Paula felt happy and optimistic.

'I want to be with you more than anyone,' she told him.

But it was only the next evening that she realised exactly how painful parting from him would be.

CHAPTER SIX

'This is awful,' Mike groaned as he reached around the steering-wheel to kiss her again.

Paula lifted her head for his kiss, but she shivered as their lips touched. They'd been parked outside her house for so long that the car was growing cold. Rain beat on the windscreen and ran down the glass.

'Mike, I'll have to go in. The lights are on.

Mandy is waiting for me.'

He looked into her eyes with his honest blue gaze.

'I didn't know it would be so hard to let you go.'

'It's only for a night.'

He shook his dark head in reply and ran one finger down her cheek.

'A lifetime.'

Paula felt herself melting.

'If only we could talk during the day or have lunch together tomorrow.'

Mike kissed her.

'That's too long to wait. I'll come and get you early in the morning. I know a place that does a great American breakfast.'

'I'll look forward to it,' Paula replied.

Mike drew back and looked at her sadly.

'Until six o'clock, then?'

It felt all wrong to pull herself away from Mike and leave him. This was no way to run a marriage. She wanted to watch him drive away but it was too wet to stand on the pavement, so Paula scurried down the path and let herself into the building and went upstairs to her flat. A trail of clothes, shoes, books, magazines and CD covers led from the hall to the front room. A lanky blonde teenager looked up from the couch.

'Hi, Auntie Paula!'

'Hi! It's lovely to see you, but you'll have to turn that music down.'

Mandy sighed, but she reached for the remote control.

'How's my favourite maiden aunt?'

'I'm fine, thank you,' Paula lied.

She couldn't resist walking over to the window and peering through her wooden venetian blinds. Mike's car was still there. She waved down into the darkness and his lights flashed briefly in reply. She was close to tears. If only she could rush outside and be with him. Mandy was curious.

'Is someone out there?'

Paula decided to be as truthful as possible.

'I've met a nice man called Sebastian. He brought me home.'

'Cool! Is it serious?'

'I've only known him a week! Well, just over a week now.'

'Way to go, Auntie Paula! Love at first sight. I can't imagine you having a mad crush on anyone.'

Cold panic swept over her. Was that all it was? An adolescent crush? It took every bit of her willpower to push aside her turbulent emotions and speak to her niece calmly.

'How are you?'

Mandy attempted a bright tone, but Paula noticed a shadow in the young girl's eyes as she answered.

'Oh, cool. You know.'

Useless to expect the teenager to tell her more, Paula realised but she knew in her heart that she'd made the right decision to have Mandy to stay.

'Well, you can stay here as long as you like. You know that.'

This time Mandy jumped off the sofa and clung to Paula in a tight hug that told her louder than any words how much her niece needed to be here, even though all that the girl actually said was, 'What's for dinner, Auntie Paula? I'm like, so hungry I could faint.'

Paula lay awake long into the night, staring at the ceiling. She was torn between her family, her friends, her career, her old steady, stable life and her new husband. As she fell asleep around three o'clock she was longing for the peace and stability of her old life. True, there had been no big highs, no whirlwind passion to whip her off her feet and carry her up to paradise, but there had been no big panics either. She'd never felt so beset by troubles.

But at six o'clock, as she stumbled out sleepily into the cold, wet morning and saw Mike waiting for her, she wouldn't have changed places with a lottery winner. It was still a surprise to see her good-looking beach bum all buttoned up in a suit. Her heart filled with such a rush of love when she saw him that she knew he was worth any amount of trouble, and from the love that blazed from his blue eyes she could see that he felt the same. He opened his arms wide.

'Come here, wife!'

They kissed on the pavement until the rain ran down their faces. Finally, Mike came to his senses.

'Darling, you're wet through. Quick, get in the car!'

'I don't care!' Paula said recklessly.

She never wanted to be parted from him again, but Mike insisted.

'I'd never forgive myself if you caught a cold!'

He put the car heaters on full and made sure they had the table by the heater in the breakfast bar. Paula had never had such a delicious breakfast, nor had the time ever gone as quickly. It felt as if they had to leave almost at once. Mike stared at her in anguish.

'It wouldn't be so bad if I could contact you at work, but it would be instant dismissal for both of us if they traced the call.'

'My Mackenzie is security mad,' Paula said. 'He monitors everything.'

'You must start job hunting.'

She could see by the expression in his eyes that she hadn't got through to him as she replied with a touch of impatience.

'I'd be lucky to find anything that paid better. My last promotion was a pretty good one.'

'So was mine.'

Mike looked at the clock that hung over the cash register and screamed. Paula followed his gaze and screamed louder. In the mad scramble that followed there was no chance to talk further, but the sense that the problem hadn't gone away felt like a heavy stone in her chest that she carried all day, until about three o'clock in the afternoon when there was a special delivery for her. She unwrapped the parcel and found a brand-new mobile phone. Mike had already registered it for her, and there was a text message waiting for her.

CAN'T WAIT FOR TONITE. CALL ME. I LUV U! xxx M.

Her heart melted as she sneaked off into the ladies to ring him back. With a love like theirs, surely they could overcome all the problems life seemed determined to throw at them.

Her sense of optimism held until late that night as she lay awake in her lonely bed, listening to the thump of Mandy's stereo in the front room. She turned over restlessly and flung out her arms. The spare two inches in her narrow bed seemed to stretch out like the empty reaches of space. She should be sleeping next to her husband. It was all wrong for a newly-married couple to be apart, and she shouldn't be telling lies to everyone, especially her mother. She'd only spoken to her briefly since she got back because she felt so guilty.

Paula felt hot and Mandy's music had changed into a tune that was incredibly irritating. The next thing would be the neighbours complaining about the noise, and who could blame them? Paula turned over again and thumped the crumpled pillow. She supposed she should start job hunting. But she knew why she was reluctant. Mike's cool assumption that she would be the one to give up her job had rankled. He didn't even know what she did. At the very least they should sit down and discuss it. But they had so little time together.

She turned over again. If only she was in his arms now. Sleep was further away than ever. She'd better count sheep. Paula made a determined effort to visualise fluffy white sheep jumping over a gate, but number five crashed into the gate with a loud knocking noise. A chill panic prickled its way down Paula's spine. That noise had been real. She was wide awake again. She lay tense and unmoving in the bed, her ears on full alert, listening as hard as she could. There was nothing. Perhaps it had been Mandy crashing around the flat, or perhaps she'd imagined the noise. All was quiet now.

Then she heard the knocking again, a tap, tap, tapping at her window. At the first tap Paula went cold with fright, but at the second she relaxed, and by the third she was smiling. She didn't know how he'd managed to reach her third-floor window, but she was pretty certain that when she sat up she wouldn't find a burglar or a moonlighting window cleaner. She could still feel herself smiling as she jumped out of bed and pattered across the bedroom to open the window. A gust of cold, damp air flowed in, followed by Mike's dark head and shoulders. She couldn't help laughing out loud when she saw he was wearing a dark sweatsuit and a black balaclava.

'Idiot!'

He swung his legs over the windowsill and stood up. Then he pulled off his ridiculous headgear and shook out his hair, blue eyes sparkling.

'Is that any way to greet your hero?'

'Mike, what if someone saw you? They might ring the police.'

He spoke with supreme confidence.

'They'll never see through my camouflage!'

Paula shook her head.

'You look like a very shady character to me.'

She couldn't resist peeking out of the window into the mist. A long, metal ladder gleamed silver in the yellow light from the street lamp.

'Where did you get a ladder at this time of night?'

'I picked it up at lunchtime from one of those tool-hire places. Now, come here, wife! There's a very good reason I went to all this trouble.'

She pressed her face to his cool skin.

'Mike, you could have been killed.'

'It's worth it, for you,' he answered coolly.

She nestled against him.

'Oh, Mike. Why is everything so difficult?'

He held her tight.

'You're the best thing that ever happened to me, and I'm not going to lose you.'

'You don't think it was just the exotic location?'

He tipped up her chin and looked directly into her eyes.

'It wasn't the location that was exciting, it was what we discovered within ourselves.'

Paula longed to believe him, but her voice was a little shaky.

'It's difficult to believe in love. I've always led such a steady life.'

Mike's tone was rueful.

'Me, too. I've spent a lifetime being sensible. I planned my career like a military campaign. I've never made a move without thinking about it over and over and then you blasted into my life like an explosion.'

He kissed her. Paula felt all the magic, but could she believe it?

'I'm nobody's dream,' she murmured sadly.

'You're mine! You're everything I've ever wanted in a woman.'

The love in his eyes carried Paula into a new realm.

'I thought only Superman could fly up to third-floor windows.'

Mike pounced very quickly and swept her

up in his arms. He swung her around until the corners of the room whirled past in a dizzy blur. 'You can fly, too, while you're in my arms!'

He tumbled her on to the bed and flung himself down beside her. His eyes were very blue as he kissed her.

'God bless the Caribbean.'

Paula looked into his loving face.

'And God bless hurricanes.'

And they sank into a world of their own making.

CHAPTER SEVEN

'If only the morning never had to come,' Paula whispered as Mike reached grumpily for his socks.

'Can't I have a shower here?'

'Mandy will wonder why I'm having two showers.'

'Let her wonder.'

'Keep your voice down. Anyway, you'll have to go home because you don't have any clean clothes here.'

Mike buttoned up his crumpled shirt with very bad grace. Paula could feel her shoulders tensing up. Was her new husband always such a bear in the mornings? Then she reminded herself that having to climb into yesterday's clothes without a shave, a shower or breakfast was enough to sour any man. She looked up from her unhappy reflections and saw that he was watching her. The light of love was back in his eyes.

'Twenty years from now we'll laugh about this,' he promised her.

She went directly into his arms, but her voice was rueful.

'I don't think I'll ever laugh again!'

Mike kissed her, but then he pulled back and looked at her pleadingly.

'Surely your niece won't think it's too strange if you have two cups of tea in your room. I can't face the world without a hot drink!'

Paula flew to get him one, and they were both laughing as he slipped away down the ladder, collapsed it and crossed the deserted early-morning street to his car. Yet she couldn't shake off a feeling of unease that grew stronger throughout the day.

She tried to throw herself into her work, but the tension wouldn't go away. She stopped trying to make sense of the rows of figures she was supposed to be working on and sat idly at her desk, staring at the beautiful pink shell that she'd brought back with her to use as a paperweight.

On impulse, she picked up the shell and pressed it to her ear. The sound of the sea beat against her eardrum. Nostalgia flooded over her. In the tropical Caribbean, warm emotions had seemed to unfold so easily. Under that vivid blue sky she'd felt humour and passion and warmth blossoming as riotously as the purple bougainvillea that had tumbled over the church where they'd married. But back in grey England she was becoming tense and overwrought and she knew it. The magic was fading but she was filled with a fierce determination to save her marriage.

She and Mike had a love worth fighting for, but how could they keep their relationship alive when they were pulled at from so many directions? And he was furious when she wouldn't go out with him that evening.

'This is insane!' he declared as they drove home together.

'Mandy rang the office and said she was making spaghetti for me. I can't leave her alone on her first night.'

'You left me alone last night.'

'But not for long. You made sure of that.'

He refused to be mollified.

'How long are we going to maintain this double-sided nonsense?'

'Until one of us finds a new job. Have you written out a CV yet?'

His eyes were hard and unforgiving.

'No. Have you?'

'Not yet. But I'll do one this evening, if you will.'

He glared at her for so long she felt

nervous, but no way would she give in. She felt her own temper flare in response to his stubbornness.

'It's only fair that we both look, Mike. It will be quicker as well. It doubles our chances of a good job coming along.'

He looked so grim that she questioned him uncertainly.

'Mike?'

He gave a quick grin that showed his dimples and lightened his eyes.

'My wife looks gorgeous when she's in a paddy! Her cheeks go pink and her eyes flash like diamonds.'

'Flattery won't win me over.'

'No, but your commonsense has won me. We'll both make CVs and we'll both start job hunting tonight, but tomorrow you're mine. Make no mistake about that, Paula. You tell that niece of yours that you're dating your new man, Sebastian.'

Paula touched his hand briefly as he changed gear.

'Nothing will stop us being together tomorrow,' she promised him.

Mike seemed content with that, and he drove her back to her flat with no further argument and kissed her goodbye so beautifully that she knew their earlier differences were forgotten. Nevertheless, she was troubled. How many more of these differences would they have to get through before they could be together?

The next few days went smoothly, or as smoothly as they can go when you have to keep your marriage a deadly secret. On Saturday morning, Mandy decided to go home for the day. Mike arrived in an extremely good mood. His blue eyes sparkled.

'Has she really gone?'

'For sure.'

'Alone at last! Come here, wife!'

Paula went into his arms, laughing, but later as they lay cuddled up together she looked into his face and voiced her worries.

'Please don't resent her, Mike. She's no trouble at all, really.'

He gave her a hug and kissed the top of her nose.

'I've nothing against Mandy personally. How could I? We haven't even met! But this situation is driving me mad.'

'Me, too. One of us has to find a new job. It's the only answer.'

Mike nodded.

'How's the job-hunting going?' he asked.

It sounded as if he was still taking it for granted that she would be the one to move. Paula felt a prickle of resentment, but she smothered it. She didn't want to spoil their Saturday together. She tried to speak calmly.

'I've contacted some recruitment agencies.'

'Good girl. You'll need to get all the trade magazines as well.'

Did he think she didn't know how to conduct a job hunt? Hurt threatened to bubble to the surface, but again she tamped it down.

'I already do.'

He hugged her again and spoke with supreme confidence.

'Then you'll have a new job in no time at all. I'm sure anyone would want a smart cookie like you.'

'How is your job search going, Mike?'

'I've had a quick look at the advertisements, but honestly, Paula, there was nothing on offer half as good as the post I now have.'

Her voice shook a bit as she answered.

'That's exactly what I thought about my situation.'

It was difficult to meet Mike's eyes, they were so diamond bright, but Paula knew that she had to stand her ground. His expression grew blacker, and it was easy to believe that he was used to running a large department. He clearly wasn't used to being crossed. But Paula knew it was important. She'd married the man without a moment's thought as to how it would work out, but she knew that if she gave in now he'd have the ascendancy for ever. And that wasn't good for any marriage.

Mike's gaze suddenly softened and he reached for her.

'Let's not waste our precious time together.'

'It's important,' she began.

'I agree, but sweetheart, didn't I tell you it

would take a while?'

'I just want things to be normal again!' she said with a sigh.

He kissed her and she could see passion blazing in his eyes.

'What's so great about normal?'

It was difficult to resist the increasing ardour of his kisses.

'Nothing much!' she murmured, kissing him back.

They spent a blissful day together, but as evening approached and Mike took a shower and Paula took her wicked new dress out of the cupboard, she couldn't resist returning to the topic.

'You'll have to admit that a double blind date is not a normal way for a married couple to spend Saturday night!'

Mike emerged from the shower. How did he manage to look so sexy even wrapped in one of her fluffy peach towels? He reached for another peach towel and started to rub his hair dry.

'I can't think of a way out of it.'

And then he saw the dress she'd selected. His eyes blazed.

'No way are you going out dressed like that! You're practically naked!'

Paula looked in the mirror before answering. She'd deliberately dressed to kill. In fact, she'd bought a new dress as none of her old ones seemed sexy enough. She'd taken extra care with her make-up and loosened her hair into a flowing cascade.

'I look like Charlene again,' she said thoughtfully. 'I never thought she could exist in England.'

She winked at her reflection. It was interesting to think that the siren who looked back at her was as real as the conventional accountant. Mike bounded across the room and gripped her bare shoulders. Paula couldn't help being thrilled when she saw his blue gaze turn smoky with passion.

'I don't want that Mackenzie boy to see Charlene! She's mine!'

Paula wound her arms around his neck and stopped teasing him.

'I've dressed for you, silly. I don't want to be upstaged by this Georgina! She might be gorgeous, and she'll have all the money in the world for clothes and grooming. I don't want you to be tempted.'

'Never,' Mike assured her in a low throaty growl. 'Never! Never! Never!'

And his kiss showed her how just how much he was attracted to her.

When they got to the Royal Albert Hotel, Mike dropped her off in front of the entrance.

'You go in now, and by the time I've parked the car, it'll look like we arrived separately,' and Paula agreed, but as she walked into the elegant lobby of the hotel, she suddenly remembered why she was there and butterflies sprang to life in her stomach.

She'd been too busy to give much thought to this blind date, but now she was faced with getting through the evening in company with a strange man while her husband flirted with his cousin. Her mouth dried in panic and she almost ran to the nearest phone to hand in her notice. But then she remembered her mortgage and how uncertain the future was. She wasn't brave enough to face the world without a job. She'd just have to get through the next few hours as best she could.

It was a relief when a good-looking young man walked up to her and spoke in a deep and educated voice.

'I think you must be Paula Jackson.'

Paula took his hand and relaxed. He looked very young, naturally, but he also looked nice as he smiled at her with warm hazel eyes from under a floppy brown fringe. Perhaps the evening wouldn't be too dreadful.

'I forgot to arrange anything in the way of red carnations or folded newspapers. How did you know who I was?'

Nigel looked at her with deep admiration.

'It wasn't easy, actually. Dad gave me a staff photograph, but I must say you look rather different tonight, in fact, rather marvellous, if you don't mind my saying so.'

Paula didn't mind at all, but either her sixth sense kicked in or a chill in the atmosphere alerted her, and before answering she took a quick look around. Sure enough, Mike was standing directly behind her. He was glaring at his rival with such fury she felt a flurry of panic and put her hand on Nigel's arm. She had to get him out of the lobby before war broke out.

'Shall we go upstairs?'

Someone had taught him lovely manners. He turned to escort her and smiled down at her nicely.

'I'm sorry. The lobby's not the most suitable place for a conversation.'

They delayed for a few minutes while Nigel consulted with a personage in gold braid and a wonderful uniform. The hotel employee even spoke in a stately manner.

'If sir and madam would care to follow me to the lifts.'

He ushered them into a fantastic old lift with gold-mirrored walls. Iron doors clanged shut behind them, and Paula saw that the mirrors were throwing back a myriad reflections of her in her brand new dress and glittering evening coat. She smiled at Nigel's reflection and wondered what Rory Mackenzie was worrying about. Nigel looked like a thoroughly nice young boy.

Then she felt as if she'd been punched in the stomach as she took in the reflection of Mike's towering figure standing just behind her. What bad luck that he was in their lift. She met his gaze and swallowed hard. He was ignoring his date and glaring at her. She read the warning in his dangerous blue eyes and shivered. The lift creaked and whirred and began its ascent to the top floor. Paula wished it would go faster. She wanted to get out of the enclosed space before the smouldering volcano of Mike's temper erupted.

Feeling curious about his date, she sneaked a sideways peek at the slender young girl next to her husband. The first thing she noticed was Georgina's auburn hair, then how freshly tanned her brown skin was, then how skimpy her bright red clinging dress looked. Georgina had noticed she wasn't alone in the lift. She was staring at Nigel with a look of mingled glee and derision.

'It's Nige boy! And you're still spotty!' she shrieked in a voice that could shatter glass tumblers.

Nigel gave a theatrical wince.

'And Decibel Mackenzie still hasn't learned how to use the volume control.'

Georgina gave him a venomous look.

'Picked up some lovely manners in Paris, did you, Nige, dear?'

He regarded her evenly.

'I learned how to tell a lady from a spoiled brat.'

As the exchange of insults continued, Paula rolled her eyes to the mirrored lift ceiling in despair. No chance of the children in this family quarrel getting together and healing the breach! Then she let out a startled squeak as a hand firmly gripped her bottom and Mike growled in her ear.

'Remember, I'll be keeping an eye on you. No batting your lashes at the Mackenzie boy.'

Her cheeks felt hot and she knew she was blushing, but fortunately the Mackenzie cousins were still too busy abusing one another to notice. A brass bell dinged and the whole lift compartment bounced as they arrived at the top floor. Paula gave in to a wicked impulse and fluttered her lashes at Mike. Her whisper was soft and silky and pitched for him alone.

'What fun would it be not flirting?' she enquired softly.

Nigel took her arm and she shimmied out of the lift, deliberately exaggerating her walk for Mike's benefit. The restaurant, which took up the whole top floor of the hotel, was themed around the days of the Raj. Potted palms and magnificent mahogany furniture gleamed under crystal chandeliers and peacock feather fans. Nigel and Paula were met by the best-trained waiter she'd ever encountered, who ushered them to their table as if he really cared.

'Paula, I say, would you like a drink?'

Paula realised that Nigel was trying to get her attention. She stopped craning her neck to see where Mike and Georgina were sitting and took in the young stranger smiling anxiously at her across the table. She was going to need a stiff drink to get through the evening.

'Oh, a cocktail of some kind, please. A strong one.'

The soft-footed waiter was back within seconds, bearing a frosted pink glass that sported a bunch of cherries and an umbrella. As he put the cocktail down in front of Paula. Mike walked past. He glanced at her drink, and she distinctly heard him give a small snort. He'd drunk plenty of cocktails while they were on holiday, she mused, admiring the width of his shoulders as she watched his retreating back. Was he the kind of man who only drank beer while he was in England? It was incredible how little she knew about him.

'Hello? Paula? Would you like to see the menu?'

Paula apologised and took the red-bound menu. She vowed to concentrate on her date, who must be thinking she was half-witted by now, but within a few seconds her attention was distracted again, this time by what looked like a familiar face peering at her from behind a potted palm two tables away. She stared incredulously. That round pink face looked awfully like Rory Mackenzie! Then she shook her head.

Her boss might be mad enough to set up a blind date for his son, but he wasn't mad enough to tail him to the restaurant as well, and besides, Rory Mackenzie didn't wear glasses. She became aware that Nigel was making conversation and tried to concentrate.

'They've got some jolly different selections on this menu. I think I'll be adventurous and order the ostrich. How about you?'

Paula opened her mouth to reply, but then she spotted an auburn head that had to be Georgina's. She hated to see them together. There was no doubt about it, Paula was the jealous kind. At least, she was when it came to her husband. The pain in her heart made her wish that she hadn't teased Mike so much earlier. She had no intention of flirting with the callow youth sitting before her, but Mike didn't know that, and as if in retaliation, his dark head was awfully close to the red-headed one beside him. They seemed to be getting on very well.

'Go on!' Nigel urged. 'Be daring. Try something different.'

'Steak,' Paula said firmly.

Nigel looked a bit disappointed.

'I've had my new experience for the month,' Paula told him, though she knew the remark would sail right over his head. 'I don't need another one.'

She took another look at the other side of the restaurant. The dark head was still very close to the auburn one. She picked up her drink and drained it in one gulp. Nigel looked faintly startled, but his manners held.

'Would you care for another cocktail?'

'Yes, please!'

But she drank the next one a little more slowly! As the food arrived, Paula realised that Nigel was easy to keep happy. She asked him a few questions about modern art and Paris, and he was off. He was young enough to talk about himself the whole evening, but he was nice enough not to be a complete bore, even if she did hear more than she wanted to about the artwork of his current heroes.

Unfortunately, his monologue left her free to keep watch on the table on the other side of the restaurant. She felt a pain in her heart every time the heads moved together as if Mike and Georgina were laughing. She should give in her notice and to pot with a career. This was a dreadful way to spend an evening. Paula felt as if she couldn't bear another minute. She threw down her sweet spoon and got to her feet.

'Excuse me a minute.'

Nigel stood up and looked embarrassed.

'Of course. Is there anything . . .'

Paula shook her head.

'Just a trip to the powder room.'

Nigel looked relieved and sat down. Paula made for the ladies' room. On the way, she tried to take another look at the man who'd reminded her of Rory Mackenzie, but his head was buried in the menu.

I was imagining it, she told herself, and turned down the palm-lined corridor that led to the cloakrooms. They were incredibly grand, with wicker sofas and huge, carved elephants dotted around. On the way back, she caught the gleam of eyes in the undergrowth and for a horrified second she thought one of the carved elephants was looking at her, but elephants don't have blue eyes.

'Mike! You'll knock the plants over!'

The gleam in his blue eyes deepened.

'Never mind the plants! Come here!'

'I can't!'

She hadn't meant it as a challenge, but she saw the spark of combat light up his face.

'Then I'll come and get you.'

He'd never back down, and now she heard voices and laughter as a party of restaurant customers entered the corridor on their way to the cloakrooms. She had a split second to decide. She pushed aside the spicy-smelling fronds of a big weeping fig plant and joined Mike behind his carved elephant. His arms went around her. Paula's freshly-applied lipstick went west. She distinctly heard footsteps and realised people were only a few inches away. In a panic they'd be discovered, she crouched farther down under the sheltering leaves of the potted plants, hoping the wooden elephant was big enough to conceal her.

'Mike,' she hissed. 'We're in the Royal Albert Hotel!'

'I don't care what people think, I just want to kiss you! Do you know what agony it is to see you looking so happy with that weasel of a Mackenzie?'

She kissed him with feeling, then replied, 'Do you think I like seeing you with Georgina?'

There was all the passion in the world in his eyes.

'Tell me you love me!'

She wound her bare arms around his neck and didn't care who saw them. If her boss walked past now she'd throw her resignation at his head.

'I love you! I love you! I love you!' she cried.

The ferns rustled around them. If only they were alone in a tropical jungle, but they weren't, and at last Paula spoke reluctantly.

'We shouldn't be doing this.'

'Married folks do it all the time, but our dates will be wondering where we are.'

'We've been away too long, right enough.'

But Paula didn't want to go back to the table.

'Mike, I don't want to go back to work, and work is all it is, Mike. Don't let's tease one another any more. It's just a part of the job.'

Paula made her way back to her table. She'd thrown aside her sober, well-organised life so fast that it might never have existed. Look at her now! She'd loved every minute of their stolen kiss. She could see Mike's dark figure moving towards Georgina's table and from the set of his shoulders she knew he was smiling, just as she was.

She'd risk anything for the heady pleasure of being in Mike's arms. Then she remembered how long she'd been away and felt guilty. It had been very rude of her to leave Nigel for so long. Her lips were framing excuses when she got to the table, but Nigel's seat was empty.

Baffled and horrified, she took a hasty look around the restaurant. There was a cold feeling in her stomach. Surely he hadn't got tired of waiting and gone home without her. It seemed unlikely, but where else could he be? There was no sign of him. Puzzled, Paula stared around the restaurant until an outbreak of shouting across the room attracted her attention. The noise was coming from Mike's table. Georgina was on her feet, waving a plate in the air. She looked like a fashion model in her shimmery red dress but she was screeching like a demented parrot.

At the tables nearby every head was turned as the diners took in the scene. Their faces were shocked. The Royal Albert was not the kind of place where people rowed noisily, and Paula saw that a posse of waiters was heading full speed for Mike's table. She ran after them, and saw that her missing date was sitting at Mike's table. Nigel was soaking wet and he had bits of food on his suit. As Paula watched he got slowly to his feet and confronted Georgina, who clutched her empty plate and looked defiant. Nigel looked so angry that Paula wondered how she'd ever considered him to be a nice young boy. His hazel eyes were deadly.

'You happen to be safe for the moment, dear cousin, as we are very much in public, but the next time I see you I'll put you over my knee and spank the life out of you, and that's a promise. You've had it coming for a long time.'

Georgina tossed back her hair and regarded him with defiant eyes. Her voice was so loud that just about every diner in the restaurant winced.

'You deserved to have food thrown at you for insulting me! I'm nothing like a foghorn! I'm not!'

Paula saw one of the waiters smile at that, but they still closed in on the table as smoothly as if they'd been trained by the riot police. Within seconds, Mike was leading Georgina out of the restaurant and Nigel was being patted down and dried off. Paula was only too keen to get out of the place quickly, and she brushed off his half-headed suggestion that they should go to a nightclub.

'Believe me,' she said frankly, 'all I want to do is go home.'

Nigel's cheeks flushed a little.

'I hope it wasn't too dreadful for you.'

Paula smiled at him. After all, none of this was Nigel's fault.

'Or for you. We did get rather landed with

one another,' she replied.

Nigel looked rueful as he ushered her into a taxi and got in after her.

'I'll see you home.'

He was silent for a moment then he seemed to decide to confide in Paula.

'I did try to tell Dad that you'd probably have better things to do on Saturday night than go out with an art student, but you know what he's like when his mind's made up.'

'Only too well,' Paula agreed.

She hesitated, wondering if she could trust Nigel. He seemed nice and there was no way she wanted to risk another evening like the one they'd just experienced.

'Can you keep a secret?'

Nigel nodded and looked at her with curiosity in eyes that were very much like his father's.

'Go on.'

'I've met someone, very recently, but it has to be a secret for now.'

Nigel looked at her for a moment then gave a boyish grin.

'As it happens, I'm in love with a girl myself, but for reasons I won't go into, I can't spill the beans to Dad, not just yet, anyway.'

They parted in amicable agreement and Paula waved the taxi away feeling better about life. At least she and Nigel were on the same wavelength. The flat was dark when she let herself in and Mandy wasn't home. Perhaps things were cooling down at home and the teenager would move back with her family, and then Paula would be free to spend time with her husband. She sighed and threw her coat on the chair. Her mobile phone rang. She picked it up with a smile on her lips.

'Mike! What a diabolical evening.'

'Dismal!' he agreed. 'Don't go to bed! I've got rid of the metal-voiced Georgina and I'm coming to get you.'

'Mandy might be back any minute.'

'Leave her a note, because she's going to find you gone. I want you with me tonight and I want us to spend a peaceful, relaxed Sunday together tomorrow. I'll bring you breakfast in bed and we'll sit around and read the papers. How does that sound?'

Paula closed her eyes and felt dreamy.

'Wonderful,' she answered softly. 'We need a quiet day together.'

'Just you and me,' Mike agreed. 'Hang on, baby. I'm coming to take you to paradise.'

CHAPTER EIGHT

Paula felt very much the worse for wear on Sunday morning. Mike was most unsympathetic. He shook his finger at her.

'If you will drink pink drinks with umbrellas in them.'

She groaned.

'Don't be so mean. I only had two!'

'Stay in bed. I'll make you some tea and dry toast. Do you think you could manage that?'

'Just about,' Paula told him, thinking how nice it was to be looked after, and she did feel better after she'd finished eating.

'I think I could get up now.'

Then she discovered that she'd forgotten to bring a dressing-gown.

'What would you prefer? A sheet, an old rugby shirt, or a towel?' Mike asked her.

'I'll use the sheet for now,' Paula answered, wrapping it around her until she looked like a ghost at a Halloween party. 'Where's my suitcase?'

'In the front room, I think,' Mike answered.

Yawning, she followed him through into his lounge. She'd never had time to look around the house. It was hard to believe she was married to the man who owned this room. She didn't even know what books he had on the shelves.

'What kind of music do you like?' she asked him.

At that precise moment there was a hysterical banging on the front door. Paula and Mike looked at each other. He opened his hands wide in a gesture of bafflement.

'Who could that be?'

Paula pulled up her slipping sheet.

'How should I know? It's your front door.'

Now the bell shrilled out and shrilled again as if someone were leaning on it. Mike started to look annoyed.

'This early on a Sunday morning! Who on earth . . .'

Not bothering to finish his sentence he strode across the room and went into the hall. Paula heard him yank open the front door and bellow out loud.

'What do you want?'

Then there was silence. She waited nervously, listening to the sound of her own breathing. Then she heard a tearful, female voice.

'Is that any way to greet your own mother?'

Paula felt as if she'd been knocked out by a boxer! Mike's mother! And she was standing in the middle of the front room wrapped only in a sheet. She looked around her, feeling trapped. Her clothes! Where were her clothes? She suddenly spotted her suitcase poking out from behind Mike's big leather sofa. She darted over to it and tried to lift it. Much too heavy. Holding up her sheet, she got behind it and tried to push, but before it had moved more than an inch, the door of Mike's lounge burst open and his mother charged into the room, wailing like a banshee.

'I just want you to tell me that all these terrible rumours aren't true.'

There was nothing Paula could do but dive behind the sofa and hope for the best. She clutched her sheet and buried her head in her arms, wondering if she was fated to spend the whole of her married life skulking around behind furniture! She didn't dare peep out to see what Mike's mother looked like, but you didn't need to see Mrs Kent to know she was unhappy. Her voice vibrated with outrage and self pity.

'I told James straightaway. I told him, it's got to be a lie. As if my Michael would get married without his mother being there on the big day, let alone not telling her at all.'

Paula went cold all over. Mike's friend, James, was the only other person who knew about the marriage, but she knew Mike had been to see his best man and impressed on him that the marriage was a secret, so how had the news got out? Perhaps James hadn't realised they were keeping the secret from their families. A deep male voice was making soothing noises, and Paula surmised that the bass sounds came from Mike's father. He was there, too! Then she felt a tremor run through the sofa as if Mike had flopped down on it. From the sound of his voice when he spoke, she guessed that he had his head in his hands.

'I'm really sorry, Mum.'

The screech that followed sounded like a factory fire warning.

'You mean it's true? You've been deceiving your mother! Oh, my goodness. Arthur, I'm going to have one of my attacks! Arthur!

Where are my smelling salts?'

Paula scrunched up small behind the sofa, but even in her misery she was fascinated. Smelling salts! They went out with Queen Victoria. What kind of a woman could Mike's mother be? Paula shivered. The sheet wasn't very warm. Her fingers and toes were practically frozen by the time the two men had succeeded in quietening Mike's mother to a few gasping sobs.

'I'm sorry, Mum,' she heard Mike say. 'Let me introduce you to Paula and explain how it all happened. You'll understand when you hear the whole story.'

'To think a son of mine could be so deceitful!'

There was a prolonged silence, but Mrs Kent didn't make any other protest, which Mike seemed to take as permission to introduce his bride. His tone was cheery as he called out.

'Paula? Where are you, my darling? I'd like you to meet my mother.'

For a moment, Paula contemplated staying hidden behind the settee, but she was cold and cramped and she didn't hold out any hope that she could outstay Mike's parents, so she gripped her sheet with trembling hands and crawled out into view. Mike's parents sat bolt upright on their chairs and gazed at her with identical expressions of shock. They looked exactly like their voices. Mr Kent was homely,

97

dressed in corduroy trousers and a baggy cardigan. Mrs Kent was formally magnificent in a blue suit. Neither of them spoke to Paula, and Mike seemed to have been struck dumb by the sudden appearance of his bride from behind the sofa.

'I was just, ah, getting something out of my suitcase,' Paula said.

Mr Kent was the first to recover. He got out of his armchair and walked over to Paula, kindly pretending not to notice the sheet and her tangled hair. He gave her a kiss on one cheek and said in hearty tones, 'Well, it's very nice to meet you, my dear.'

Paula looked timidly into his face and saw that his eyes were kind. Mrs Kent was icy and unforgiving.

'Am I to believe that you are married to my son?'

Mike and Paula looked at each other guiltily. She let Mike do the talking.

'Well, kind of. Yes, I suppose so.'

'And might I enquire how this came about?'

Mike fell silent again, but Paula couldn't blame him. How could anyone possibly explain crazy passion to this iceberg on the sofa? Mike made a valiant effort to explain what had happened.

'We sort of met on holiday and then we kind of fell in love.'

Mrs Kent snorted.

'Marriage is a serious business. It needs

planning and preparation.'

Mike flushed but he faced his mother steadily.

'It was love at first sight, Mother.'

She lifted one chilly eyebrow and Paula felt all the force of the woman's character.

'I had always understood love to be something that grew slowly and steadily over time.'

Unexpectedly rescue came from Mr Kent.

'Mike's talking about love, not his investment portfolio. Young people will be young. After all, we were madly in love once, weren't we, Julia?'

Julia Kent looked as if she'd have something to say to her wayward husband on the subject of answering back when she got him home, but she settled back on the sofa and spoke with a regal air.

'You may explain the circumstances to me, Michael. You'll find that I'm not unwilling to listen.'

Paula seized her chance.

'I'll just get dressed.'

She slunk off to the bedroom, trailing her sheet behind her. She still didn't have any clean clothes. As she ransacked Mike's cupboards looking for anything suitable, she could hear him telling an edited version of their story to his parents. By the time she went back into the lounge, dressed in a warm fleece sweater and some jog pants, Mr Kent was completely won over. He looked at Paula with smiling eyes, and she could see at once that Mike had inherited the warm colour of his blue eyes from his father. Mr Kent got to his feet and this time he gave Paula a big hug and a kiss on the cheek.

'Well, don't that beat the band?' he asked her.

And then he laughed out loud and teased his son.

'I told you those sausages would get you into trouble one day! I can't believe you two work for the Mackenzie brothers!'

Mrs Kent gave a chilly smile.

'I never heard of anything so ridiculous. Paula must hand in her notice.'

Paula looked at Mike, who looked at the carpet. She would have to speak up. She cleared her throat.

'We're both looking around for something new.'

Mrs Kent rained the icy glare of her pale blue eyes on Paula, who could see at once that Mike had picked up his attitude about working females from his mother. Mrs Kent was outraged.

'You can't expect Michael to give up his job. He's doing so well at his company.'

Paula's mouth was dry, but the more she was opposed on his point, the more important she felt it was. Her voice shook and she sounded more belligerent than she'd meant to.

'Why should I be the one to give up my job? I'm successful as well, you know, and I worked hard to get where I am.'

Mrs Kent looked at her with eyes that carried no trace of understanding.

'But you'll leave anyway when you have children. Michael's always wanted two children, a boy and then a girl.'

Mr Kent came to the rescue again.

'Now then, Julia. Let's leave placing an order with the stork until these two lovebirds have finished their honeymoon.'

Children, Paula thought. She felt weak with the longing to have a little girl with Mike's blue eyes, or a boy with his heavenly dimples. She knew Mike would like children one day, but they hadn't had a minute to discuss how many or how soon. She looked at Mike's mother and tried to smile.

'We won't be discussing maternity leave just yet.'

She'd said the wrong thing again. Mike's mother looked horrified.

'I don't believe in working mothers!' she announced.

Paula had absolutely no idea how to handle the disapproving female who was sitting on the couch. She fell back on the time-honoured remedy.

'Would anyone like a cup of tea?'

'By jove, yes,' Mr Kent said, rubbing his hands together. 'You'd like a nice cup of tea, wouldn't you, Julia?'

Julia Kent didn't go so far as to agree, but she drank the tea when Paula brought it in, which seemed like no small victory. After they'd drunk their tea, and talked for a while, Mr Kent got to his feet.

'Come along now, Julia.'

'But we always have lunch with Michael on Sundays.'

Mr Kent laughed out loud.

'We'll have to share him from now on.'

Julia Kent remained stubbornly on the sofa.

'We might as well stay now that we're here.'

Paula tried to remember what food they had brought home from the supermarket and wondered how long it would take to knock up a meal, but Mr Kent crossed the room and put a determined hand under his wife's elbow. He heaved his wife to her feet and propelled her across the room. The door slammed behind them and Paula let out a huge sigh then fell flat on her back on the leather sofa. Mike pulled a rueful face. His blue eyes were sombre.

'I think that went well.'

'You do?' Paula exclaimed, sitting bolt upright.

His laugh was awkward.

'Mum's lovely, of course, but she doesn't like surprise.'

Paula had more on her mind than relatives. She held out her arms.

'I haven't kissed you for at least an hour.'

'Two hours and fifty-five minutes,' Mike returned. 'I kept watching the clock and thinking about being alone with you.'

And for the rest of the day, they behaved like that couple who fell in love on a tropical beach.

CHAPTER NINE

Monday morning came far too soon and Paula found herself sitting facing Mr Mackenzie in his office. Her peppery boss was sitting still for once, and his expression was downcast.

'I'm sorry about Saturday night. I never saw the like in my life. But you don't want to be put off. Nigel's a good lad, you know. One of the best.'

'It was you behind that potted palm!' Paula burst out in astonishment.

Rory Mackenzie looked a little abashed.

'Aye, well, I just thought I'd keep an eye on things, see how they went.'

The feeling that she'd love to be sacked gave Paula all the confidence in the world. She faced her boss and spoke sternly.

'You are being ridiculous about Nigel, and for nothing! He's a very normal young man. Stop matchmaking. He'll find himself the perfect wife when the time comes.'

Rory Mackenzie looked at her with hazel eyes, just like his son's.

'Did you think so?'

'I do!' Paula said firmly.

Her boss heaved a deep sigh.

'His mother says you can't put an old head on young shoulders, but I don't know. Seems to me the lad doesn't take sausages seriously enough. Not that folk seem to take anything seriously these days. You used to be able to depend on the Royal Albert. I never saw the like of that menu! Kangaroo! Rattlesnake! I don't know what the world's coming to.'

The glimmer of an idea knocked at the back of Paula's mind.

'People are much more adventurous about food these days,' she said slowly, wondering if Rory Mackenzie would be interested in her thoughts. 'Perhaps we could make our sausages tie in with that feeling. Not just new recipes, but a themed range, something that sounded really exciting. Safari Sausages, say!'

All Rory's pep returned. He bounced upright in his chair. His words came out in an excited splutter.

'I can see it all! Campfires under the stars. Game prowling around the camp. The smell of wood smoke. By George, I can see it all.'

He looked at Paula and gave her a big, warm smile from under his eyebrows.

'I've always said you had a good head on your shoulders, and this proves it, and you know the business from the bottom up. My mind's made up, yes it is. That James Cole put his notice in today. Going to America, he is. How would you like to be my next Finance Director?'

Paula was stunned.

'Aye, that's surprised you! But I mean it, you know.'

'When is James leaving?'

'He's left. I told him to clear out his desk today. Oh, I'll pay him his wages, but I don't hold with ex-employees on the premises. I don't know where his loyalties might lie now, and I'm not a man to take any chances with security.'

Paula closed her eyes and felt dizzy.

'Can I have time to think about your offer?'

Rory chuckled.

'If you insist, but I know what you'll say in the end. You'll do it. You were made to do this job, girl. I don't care what anybody says about your age, no I don't. You've a smart head on your shoulders and you'll make a great Finance Director.'

All through the rest of the day, Paula kept wondering if she'd imagined the conversation with her boss. It didn't seem real, and yet there was a warm glow inside her that acknowledged the truth of Rory Mackenzie's words. She loved her work and she knew she did it well. Finance Director was a big step, but she was longing to take it. What an achievement. She couldn't wait to tell Mike the exciting news.

They met in the Tapas Bar after work. Their waiter brought them plates of baked fish and a delicious seafood salad. Paula lifted her glass of dry Mexican beer and faced her new husband.

'How was your day?' she asked.

Mike lit up like a Christmas tree. He glowed with happiness.

'Terrific! You'll never guess! I've been appointed to the board!'

Paula was thrilled.

'That's amazing! They must think the world of you. Tell me about it.'

Mike laughed merrily and his eyes sparkled. He reached out and grasped her hand as he spoke.

'Thank you for insisting I look for a new post. Old Mackenzie caught me job-hunting. He doesn't want me to go, so he came up with this package. Wow! I can't believe it! Me a director! At my age!'

'We should order champagne. I've had good news today as well.'

Mike ordered the champagne, but he hardly seemed interested in Paula's promotion. He twisted the top off the bottle and poured out the foaming bubbles. Paula forced a smile as they clinked their frosted glasses together. She willingly drank to Mike's splendid news, but she wanted him to acknowledge her own. But when she tried to tell him about her promotion, he gave her a careless hug.

'But, darling, it doesn't matter. There's no need for you to work now I'm a director. I'll buy a big house and you can stay home and decorate it.'

The champagne tasted bitter in her mouth and the bright, smoky bar seemed to blur as she looked around her.

'Aren't we even going to talk about it?'

Mike's blue eyes were baffled and his tone was impatient.

'What's to discuss? Haven't you been listening? I've been made a director and all our worries are over.'

'It seems to me that they're only just beginning.'

Mike's face took on an irritated look.

'What's the matter? Come on, Paula, don't spoil my big day.'

She so wanted to give in, to fling herself into his arms and say, OK, we'll forget about me. But the hurt she felt was too real to allow for pretence.

'What about my big day? You haven't even congratulated me yet.'

'Congratulations.'

They sat in silence for a few minutes and Paula wondered why his congratulations hadn't made her feel better. She looked at his handsome face and wondered what was going through his mind, if he was thinking at all of how she was feeling. He gave her an excited grin.

'Where would you like to look at new houses? I've always liked Cheshire. How about you?'

Paula exerted all her self-control and forced a bright smile to her lips. Her best effort was horrible. Her voice sounded strained and unnatural.

'Cheshire sounds lovely.'

Mike looked at her curiously.

'What's wrong, Paula? I can see you're not happy.'

What a relief it was to let rip.

'You're not listening to me and you're not taking me seriously. I hate that. It makes me feel as if I don't matter.'

Mike was all wounded dignity.

'I've just asked you where you want to live.'

Paula couldn't stand it. She jumped to her feet and pushed her way through the crowded bar to get her coat. Then she stormed out into the night. Of course it was raining and there was a bitter wind blowing. She put her head down, wrapped her arms around herself and stomped down the wet street towards the bus stop. It wasn't long before she became aware that a car was following her.

'Go away!'

She was crying as she spoke. Tears mingled with the rain on her face. She broke into a run and arrived at the stop breathless. Mike pulled up seconds behind her and wound down the

108

window.

'Paula, for heaven's sake, will you get in the car?'

She turned her back on him and peered down the wet road, willing the yellow-lit windows of the bus to come into sight. The road stayed empty. The vicious wind chilled her wet face. She was thoroughly cold and miserable. The car door slammed and she heard footsteps.

'What's the matter with you?' Mike asked as he arrived at her side.

'Go away!' she said again.

The other people waiting at the stop looked at her curiously, and one large man stepped forward. He was holding a mobile phone.

'Is he bothering you? I can call the police in a second.'

Mike took no notice. He simply stepped forward and threw Paula over his shoulder in a fireman's lift. Upset as she was, she didn't want him arrested. As Mike carried her off she shouted to the passengers.

'It's all right. He's my husband.'

'Ah, love!' her would-be rescuer said.

Mike dropped her into the front seat of his car in an undignified bundle. Paula straightened her coat and pushed back her wet hair. She had to admit that it was nice to be out of the vile weather, but she didn't say so because Mike gave her one hard look and then he gunned the engine and sped down the road that led to her flat. His voice was tight and angry.

'Do you mind telling me what all this is about?'

Paula felt defeated before she even began.

'I've been trying to tell you.'

He sized her up the way adversaries have since the dawn of time.

'Go on! I'm listening.'

Paula looked at his angry profile and made a cowardly excuse.

'I can't talk to you seriously while you're driving.'

Mike's expression was furious, and he practically spat his words out between thin lips.

'When we get home, then.'

But when he pulled up at her flat, all the lights were on and even from the street they could hear Mandy's music. Mike thumped the steering-wheel.

'This is ridiculous. Come on, we're going back to my place.'

The more he bossed her around, the more stubborn Paula felt.

'How about discussing where we go next?' she suggested.

Mike's temper was simmering nicely.

'What's to discuss? We can't talk in your place, that's for sure.'

'Well, no, but you make these sweeping decisions without consulting me or even asking me what I want.'

She'd never seen such an unfriendly face.

'What do you want, Paula?'

She turned her head and stared out blindly into the wet night.

'I wish we'd never left Rum Smugglers' Cove.'

His voice was full of anger.

'That's very helpful.'

She turned back to him and made a last desperate effort.

'Mike, we shouldn't talk to each other like this. Married couples should be friends. They should help one another and listen to each other and . . .'

She was crying so hard that she couldn't go on. The silence was long and dreadful. Mike's voice was so bitter she could barely stand to listen.

'Do you call this a marriage?'

Paula hurt so much that she couldn't stay in the car. She reached forward blindly and groped for the handle. Mike made no move to stop her opening the door. In fact he slammed it closed behind her. Then he drove off in a screech of tyres on the wet road. She couldn't believe he'd gone, or that he wasn't coming back.

She stood like a fool on the pavement while she was wet through and shivering violently. Slowly, reluctantly, she accepted that he wasn't coming back. She moved like an old woman as she crossed to her flat and hauled herself up the stairs. It took all her nerve to push open the door to her lounge and face Mandy. Then she saw that the teenager was hurling clothes into a suitcase. Mandy gave her a brief look, and then a longer one.

'Wow! You look like a road accident, Auntie Paula.'

Paula pushed back her dripping wet hair.

'Are you going somewhere?'

'Mum wants me home.'

'What about the boys?'

'Well, they are pretty wormlike, but I guess I'll get used to them.'

'I'm so glad it's working out.'

Forgetting her dreadful state, Paula moved forward to give Mandy a hug. Her niece warded her off.

'No way you're touching me! Get in that shower, Auntie Paula.'

Paula was only too glad to strip off her dripping wet clothes and obey. The hot water was soothing, and she thought she was getting control of herself, but Mandy brought a cup of tea into the bathroom and slid it under the shower curtain and the clumsy teenage gesture of concern made her burst into tears again. She was still in the shower when her sister arrived to collect Mandy. Clare sang out.

'I can't stay. I've left the others in the car and they'll be halfway to London if I stop to talk. When are you coming round?'

'Soon,' Paula promised.

The sound of the running shower must have masked the wobble in her voice, because Clare seemed satisfied and ran off down the stairs taking Mandy with her. Paula turned off the water. An aching silence descended on the flat. Paula reached for one of her embroidered towels but a vision of Mike wrapping the peach towel around his tanned hips returned to haunt her and she sank to the floor in tears. She hurt all over and she'd never been so confused in her life. Was she married or not?

She finally pulled herself together and staggered into the kitchen. She heated up a tin of soup, thinking that she ought to eat, but it tasted like cotton wool in her mouth and she let the spoon fall listlessly. She kept looking at the phone Mike had sent her, but it stubbornly refused to ring.

She lay awake most of the night listening to the rain drumming on the roof and starting every time she heard a sound outside that might be a ladder arriving at her window. But it never was.

Her phone didn't ring the next day, or the next either. Paula dragged herself around the office on automatic pilot and cried her way through the long evenings at home. She'd known marrying Mike was a reckless thing to do, but no amount of premeditation could have led her to imagine such a dreadful ending to their relationship.

She couldn't believe that he wasn't going to ring her, but as one week stretched into two, she began to realise that her marriage was over. And then she woke up one morning feeling horribly sick. As soon as she could leave the bathroom, Paula raced for her personal organiser and began counting the days. She didn't need to use a calculator to come up with the answer. She was pregnant!

She was certain in her own heart that she was having a baby, but just to make sure she stopped off on the way to work and went to the chemist. Then she locked herself into the biggest cubicle in the ladies' room at work before trying the test. Despite all her suspicions, seeing the results for real was a shock. She read all the instructions again. There was no mistake. The indicator said she was pregnant. Paula stared at it blankly. The situation overwhelmed her. She couldn't get through this alone. She reached for her mobile, but the number she dialled wasn't Mike's.

'Mum? Mum? Will you be in tonight?'

She felt like a child again as she listened to the reply.

'Am I going to find out why you've been avoiding me since you got home?'

'Oh, Mum, I'm sorry.'

She heard a chuckle in the reply.

'Does it have anything to do with a handsome young man you've been seen with in

114

the supermarket?'

'Oh, Mum, it's all gone wrong.'

Her mother spoke more soberly.

'Don't worry about it until tonight. You can tell me all about it then.'

Paula had hoped that she'd feel better after talking to her mother, but once she'd spilled out the whole tale, she felt worse than ever. She looked pleadingly at her mother, who sat across from her at the familiar kitchen table, sipping her tea, and looking back at her with love in her eyes.

'So it's over? Well, darling, it's probably a good thing, seeing as this Mike has turned out to be such a selfish brute.'

Paula touched the wedding ring that hung on its leather bootlace under her blouse.

'He's not a brute! And he's not selfish at all, really. It's just that he didn't seem to care a bit about my career.'

Her mother shook her head gravely.

'Well, that's no good in a husband. I think it's fantastic that you've been made Finance Director. You'll be able to afford a nanny now. You can easily bring up the child by yourself. Who needs a man?'

Paula looked at her mother and wondered why a smile was lurking around the corners of her mouth.

'But I've heard you say a million times that you could never have brought us up alone.'

Her mother didn't seem to be listening. Her

eyes were dreamy.

'My youngest baby is going to be a mother herself. I can't believe it. My little Paula!'

'Do you think I'll be able to manage? Look how hard Clare found life after her husband left.'

Her mother smiled.

'But your character is very different from your sister's. Clare needs a man to lean on. Even when you were a little girl you liked to be in total command. "Me do!" you used to say. "Paula do it mine self."'

Paula felt as if she'd been insulted.

'Are you saying that I'm a control freak?'

That smile at the corners of her mother's mouth deepened.

'Don't be silly. But I think you're right to concentrate on your career. You'll be fine on your own with a baby. You'd do nothing but argue with a bossy boots like Mike.'

'We didn't argue that much. It was only about my job.'

'So he wouldn't listen and you left him. What's the problem?'

Paula burst into tears.

'I miss him so much.'

Her mother passed a large handkerchief and sat watching quietly while Paula had her cry.

'I don't want to be on my own. I want Mike back.'

'So go talk to him. Get him to listen, or at

least find out why he's being so dense about your job.'

Paula thought of the chilly Mrs Kent.

'I already know. His mother's dead against working women. He's probably soaked up her attitude without realising it. But I will talk to him. I have to. I can't stand life without him.'

Paula's mother smiled.

'Give me a hug, darling, and do cheer up. Actually, Mike sounds absolutely perfect for you and I can't wait to meet him.'

'But you said . . .' Paula began in astonishment.

Her mother gave an impish grin.

'Would you have listened, half an hour ago?'

Paula reflected on the devious nature of mothers as she stood at the train station. She put a hand over her perfectly flat stomach. The thought that she'd soon be a mother was deeply exciting. The train pulled in with a screech and a whoosh of cold air. Paula found a seat and mulled over her plan of action all the way back to the city.

She slept well that night, and woke up in the morning still perfectly resolved to put in her notice. It was no use being in perfect control of a meaningless life. The idea of letting go scared her silly, but Mike was worth any risk. What a letdown it was to find Mr Mackenzie's office empty. His secretary said that he was out at a trade fair and would be back after lunch.

'I can't wait until after lunch!' Paula

announced.

She tore off a sheet of paper and scribbled out her resignation. The secretary's mouth gaped open.

'He'll go through the roof!'

'Let him!' Paula said coldly.

Then she softened.

'It's not your fault I'm quitting, but he'll want to yell at someone. I'll give him my mobile phone number.'

The secretary took the letter reluctantly, but as she scanned the words on the page she let cut a shriek of excitement.

'You're married! Oh, my goodness! When? How come you didn't tell anybody? I'll have to start a collection! I can't believe it! What do you want for a wedding present? Can I tell the others? They'll die when they find out! I'm so excited! When did you get married? What's he like?'

Paula was laughing so much she could hardly reply.

'He's gorgeous, of course! We met and married in the Caribbean and then we got back and found we worked for the Mackenzie brothers and had to keep it a secret. You don't know how wonderful it is to be able to shout out the news.'

She reached up behind her neck and undid the bootlace that held her wedding ring.

'I don't have to hide my ring any more.'

The secretary watched Paula slipping on the

gold band.

'It's lovely, but, Paula, I'll miss you.'

'I'll miss you, and everyone, and my job, but I know what has to come first in my life.'

There was envy in the secretary's eyes.

'I don't blame you. I never heard anything so romantic in my life.'

Even though she'd given in her notice, Paula decided to respect Rory's paranoia and wait until she was off the premises before she tried to contact Mike. She felt a little strange as she went around her office sweeping her personal items into a cardboard box, but she felt even more liberated. The grey sky that had met her that morning was lifting, and as she left the main entrance of the factory for the last time, the sun came out in a golden glow.

Her gold ring glittered in the sunshine and Paula's heart was light. As she waited for her bus, she noticed that the buds on the trees that lined the street were going green. Spring wasn't far away. The mobile phone in her pocket rang. Rory Mackenzie no doubt. She was so sure that it would be her boss on the line, that it took a few seconds to place the voice in her ear.

'Mike?'

There was an awkward pause.

'Yeah. Paula, we need to talk, but not on the phone. Can we meet up some place?'

He sounded so chilly and serious that her heart started to hammer and her palms went damp. Surely he wasn't going to ask for a divorce. She answered warily.

'How about the Tapas Bar?'

'Could you do lunch?'

'I'm on my way.'

Paula broke the connection and stared blindly at the sunny street. All her optimism and thoughts of budding spring had vanished. She knew so little about the man she'd married. He could easily have decided to cut his losses. Divorce would be simple. There would be no embarrassing explanations because most people didn't even know they were married.

She picked up her cardboard box, which felt as if it was full of bricks now, and crossed the street to wait for a bus going in the other direction. By the time she got to the Tapas Bar she felt as if she were going to her execution.

Mike was waiting for her at the bar. His face was closed and unreadable.

'What do you want to eat?'

Her already nervous stomach heaved.

'Just mineral water.'

They were there before the lunchtime rush. The bar was nearly empty. They sat down at a wrought-iron table with an embarrassing scrape of chairs. Mike's voice echoed in the empty bar.

'How are you?'

'I'm fine, thank you,' she lied.

Mike was looking down at the table top.

Paula looked at his glossy black hair and ached all over with love. She wanted the right to hold him and kiss him and be with him every day, but she still didn't know what he was going to say to her. Eventually, he felt in his pocket and pushed a sheet of photocopied paper at her.

'Read this.'

A shock ran over her that stung like ice water. Had he taken out divorce papers already? Paula was reluctant to take such an official-looking document, but she couldn't sit frozen for ever, so she reached out and took the white paper with shaking hands. It was an effort to focus on the words that were written there, and when she did, Paula couldn't believe that she'd read them correctly. She looked up at her handsome husband and whispered softly.

'You're turning down the director's job? Mike, what for?'

At last he lifted his head and looked at her. As Paula saw the love and the pain and the sincerity in his kingfisher-blue eyes, her heart turned over and she knew that she'd love this man for ever. He reached across the table and took both of her hands between his before he answered.

'Because I love you. It's simple. What does a seat on the board of Sizzling Sausages mean to me if I don't have you?'

Paula felt herself melting, then laughter took hold of her in a joyous flood.

'I didn't bring you a photocopy, but, oh, Mike, guess what I did today?'

He threw back his head and laughed out loud when she told him.

'We're both unemployed?'

Paula met the love in his eyes.

'Who cares?'

Mike was looking at her as if he wanted to eat her up.

'Not me. We can sell my house and live on the proceeds for a while. I missed you so much, Paula. Did you miss me?'

'Your place isn't sold yet,' she told him softly, 'and we have no jobs to go to. Let's make the most of it.'

Their afternoon was magical, and when the moment was right, back at his place, Paula told Mike the incredible news about the baby. His eyes were soft with wonder as he touched her still-flat waistline.

'We've created a new life together. It feels like a miracle.'

Paula slipped her own hand over his.

'It is a miracle.'

Mike turned so that he could put his arms around her. Paula leaned against his chest and felt as if she'd come home at last. Then she tipped up her head so that she could look at him. There were laughter and tears in his eyes. As their lips met, she heard a promise in his voice.

'We'll be all right now. Together for ever.'

The smile in his eyes was magical, but before she could reply, her mobile phone shrilled. Paula pulled a wry face, but she felt as if nothing could disturb the happiness in her heart.

'It will be Rory Mackenzie this time. Shall I talk to him?'

Mike hesitated, but then he grinned as his own mobile phone started a musical beeping.

'You talk to your Mackenzie, and I'll talk to mine. I'd bet a lottery ticket that's my ex-boss on the other line.'

It was Rory, but his attitude was a total surprise to Paula.

'How about a barbecue at my house tonight? I've got one of my chefs around testing new recipes for the safari range. I bet you'd like that, hey? Your own safari sausages.'

Paula hoped she wasn't going to have to explain all over again.

'Haven't you been back to your office today? I left you a letter.'

She moved the phone away from her ear as her boss let out a snort that sounded like a hippopotamus at a waterhole.

'Some bosh about a new husband. Well, you can bring him along as well, if you like. Just get yourself over here.'

Paula spoke cautiously.

'Perhaps I didn't make it clear. I've resigned because Mike works for Sizzling Sausages.'

There was a longer pause and then another

tremendous snort.

'Well, as it happens, my brother will be at the party tonight, so I don't suppose it matters if you bring this Mike of yours. Bring him along, I say.'

'Party?' Paula questioned.

But her impatient boss had rung off. She turned to Mike. He was staring at his silent phone with a baffled expression. Then he looked at her with a smile full of incredulity.

'I can't believe this. Old Mackenzie is going to a barbecue at Rory's house!'

'And we're invited,' Paula told him. 'Do you want to go?'

His blue eyes were loving and tender.

'It's completely up to you. I've quit, remember?'

Paula laughed.

'So have I, but the situation intrigues me. And there's only one way to find out what's got the Mackenzie brothers talking to each other after all this time. Did I leave anything to wear here?'

An hour later, they were outside Rory Mackenzie's imposing stone mansion. A fine rain was starting to fall. Mike turned up his coat collar and shivered. Then he put his arm around Paula.

'Won't the rain spoil the barbecue?'

'There's a marvellous conservatory at the back of the house. Rory built a grill with a stone chimney.'

A maid in a lavender overall answered the door. Paula could barely contain her curiosity as their coats were taken and they were ushered through the huge, formal rooms to the orangery that overlooked the gardens. She could smell sausages as soon as she walked in. She looked eagerly for her boss, but there were so many people milling around, chatting and drinking champagne, that she couldn't see anyone she knew. She held Mike's arm and smiled into his face.

'It's so nice to have an escort!'

'And it's nice to have a beautiful woman on my arm.'

Paula looked around her curiously. The scene looked normal enough.

'What is going on?'

The answer was only a moment away. A nice-looking young man approached Paula. She recognised his floppy fringe and hazel eyes at once.

'Nigel! How are you?'

'On cloud nine, thank you. Paula, I don't think you've met my fiancée, Georgina.'

Paula felt her mouth drop open as Nigel was joined by a beautiful young woman with auburn hair.

'Hi, Mike,' she said cheerfully, and quietly. 'Nice to meet you, Paula.'

Paula felt absolutely bowled over. An engagement was the last thing she'd expected. The last time she'd seen these two together in public, Georgina had been throwing food at Nigel! Then she felt herself beginning to smile. What a wonderful end to the story.

'And Rory and his brother are actually talking to one another?'

Nigel laughed.

'Not quite! But see for yourself. Here they come.'

Rory Mackenzie had spotted Paula. He barged his way through the crowds towards her, brandishing a sausage on a long barbecue fork. He was closely followed by his wife who seemed to be keeping a sharp eye on the peace process. The first set of Mackenzies was followed by a man who looked exactly like Rory. His own wife was only a step behind him. Paula smiled as the assorted party of Mackenzies reached her. Rory blew out his cheeks and bellowed.

'What kept you? Come along now, come along. Taste this jungle sausage and tell me what you think.'

Paula took a nibble.

'It's delicious, but aren't I sacked?'

Rory's brother turned to his nephew and bawled.

'Nigel, tell your father that if he fires Paula she can come and work for me.'

Rory gave one of his tremendous snorts and yelled at Georgina.

'Now, then, young lady, you tell that father of yours to think twice before he tries to poach my best staff.'

The brothers glared at one another furiously, but the two wives moved in smoothly. Each took the arm of her husband and smoothly propelled him away. Nigel grinned ruefully, then he put an arm around his fiancée and smiled down at her.

'It'll take them a while to make friends, Georgina.'

She smiled back blissfully and answered in her new, quiet voice.

'The first grandchild will bring them around.'

The young couple drifted away to talk to their other guests, leaving Mike and Paula looking at each other in wonder. A maid walked past carrying a silver tray full of champagne flutes. Mike grabbed two glasses, then he drew Paula into the shelter of some leafy green trees. The noise of the party died away, and they could have been alone together in a tropical haven. Mike offered one of the crystal glasses to Paula and looked deeply into her eyes.

'What a wonderful world it's turned out to be. Let's celebrate.'

She found it hard to believe that all her troubles were over.

'Do you think I still have a job?'

Mike's smile was warm as he raised his glass of champagne.

'To the new Finance Director of

Mackenzie's Sausages.'

She raised her glass in return and met his eyes, smiling.

'To the new Director of Sizzling Sausages.'

Mike laughed.

'We might end up as Amalgamated Sausages.'

'That would be fun,' Paula said dreamily.

She saw that Mike was wearing his wedding ring, and she lifted her hand to show him that her own gold band was in place on her finger. He lifted her hand and kissed her ring finger. His eyes were dark and serious when he looked at her.

'Never mind career! Let's drink to our marriage.'

Paula lifted her glass and watched the bubbles sparkling in the light.

'To our whirlwind marriage.'

Mike lifted his own glass in return.

'To a hasty romance that we'll never regret!'